"They chose their bait w...

Alex stared at Kane. She hadn't the foggiest idea what he meant, but from the chill in his voice, it wasn't a compliment. "What..."

"Don't play dumb, Alex. Why do you think they sent you, anyway? Why not someone from my own team or one of the senior partners?"

She shook her head. "They sent me because I had a legitimate reason to be here."

"They sent you because our esteemed leader suspected that every time I looked at you I wasn't just thinking about law." His voice was almost brutal. "Be sure to tell him for me that the bait was very attractive. But unfortunately for him, I didn't bite quite hard enough to get hooked."

Leigh Michaels held several different jobs before settling down to writing romance novels. She feels being a writer is the most perfect career for her, however, because she can be whatever her heroines are—from antique dealer to wedding consultant to architect. She can study whatever field intrigues her and not have to take any tests. And as soon as the book is done, she can change to something else altogether. "Besides," she says, "I get to fall in love with a new man every few months, too—and my husband thinks it's great!"

Books by Leigh Michaels

HARLEQUIN ROMANCE

HARLEQUIN PRESENTS

THE LAKE EFFECT
Leigh Michaels

Harlequin Books

TORONTO • NEW YORK • LONDON
AMSTERDAM • PARIS • SYDNEY • HAMBURG
STOCKHOLM • ATHENS • TOKYO • MILAN
MADRID • WARSAW • BUDAPEST • AUCKLAND

ISBN 0-373-03275-7

Harlequin Romance first edition August 1993

THE LAKE EFFECT

CHAPTER ONE

THE RESTAURANT WAS one of the Twin Cities' newest and most upscale, and so it was always crowded at lunchtime. Today, the maître d' was turning away group after group of would-be patrons. When he saw Alexandra, however, his stern face mellowed ever so slightly into a smile. "Miss Jacobi, I'll try to find you a table right away. Will you be meeting a client?"

"No, George. I'm joining Mrs. Adler's party. The baby shower."

He nodded. "Straight through to the party room. Please give my regards to your father, won't you?"

Alex nodded. "I will—the next time I see him." She made her way slowly across the crowded restaurant, nodding to acquaintances here and there, and stopped at the door of the private dining room for half a minute, bemused by the mess and hilarity within.

She was late, of course. It wasn't her secretary's fault, for Sharon had buzzed her, as ordered, fifteen minutes before the time set for Joanna's party. But there'd been just a bit of work left to do on the case file on her desk, and that telephone call had been truly important....

The dozen young women in the party room hadn't waited for Alex, however. She hadn't expected that they would. The luncheon buffet was still set up, but the used plates had been pushed aside in favor of the main entertainment—the gaily wrapped bundles stacked in the middle of the table.

Joanna Adler looked up from the tiny stretch-terry sleeper she had just lifted from a box and said, "My word, so there still *is* an Alex Jacobi! And she's torn herself away from a law book to honor us with her presence. I'm touched to the heart, I truly am."

Alex wrinkled her nose. "Don't start on me, Joanna. You've stood me up for lunch just as many times as I have you." She picked up a plate and put a big spoonful of crab salad on it, then added a whole-wheat roll and a wedge of lettuce.

"Who has time to keep track?" Joanna pushed her chair back and crossed the room to Alex's side. Her walk was less graceful than usual, and her dress made no attempt to hide the fact that she was nearly nine months pregnant.

Alex, who hadn't seen Joanna for several weeks, couldn't keep herself from blinking in surprise.

"I know," Joanna said. "I'm as big as a boxcar. I feel like a beached whale." She gave Alex a warm hug. "If I'd known you were coming, I'd have waited to open your gift. I love it, Alex. It's precious and wonderful and I'll keep it forever—out of reach of the little darling so he can't break it."

"I'm glad you like it," Alex murmured. But her mind had gone blank. She remembered asking Sharon just a few days ago to be sure to have a gift delivered for Joanna's baby, and then she'd put the whole thing out of her mind. Had Sharon even told her what she'd chosen?

Alex spared a pang of regret for the gift she'd intended to make for this very special baby. It had seemed so simple seven months ago when Joanna had announced her happy news. More than half a year would be plenty of time for Alex to piece together one very small quilt. She had gone straight out and splurged on the materials and the pattern.

But half a year hadn't been enough, after all. Alex had underestimated her workload, and so the delicate pink-and-blue quilt still lay partly assembled and wadded up in a basket beside the sofa in her apartment. It would no doubt stay there until, in some future fit of housecleaning, she threw it away so she wouldn't be reminded of yet another good intention gone awry.

She smothered her sigh of regret. Joanna, the personnel director at an investment-banking firm, would certainly understand the way a high-pressure job could soak up time.

"I'm taking six weeks' maternity leave," Joanna was saying as she unfolded the pink wrapping paper from another box. "And I must admit I'm looking forward to just staying home for a while."

There were howls of disbelief. Alex didn't join in, but she agreed. The high-powered Joanna puttering around the house?

Joanna put her hands on her hips. "Do you know, any of you, what simple pleasure it will be not to have to wear panty hose if I don't want to? But of course you don't—none of you needs a crane to put them on in the morning!"

The maître d' appeared with a telephone. "Miss Jacobi, there's a call for you."

Alex turned her back to the laughing group.

It was Sharon, and she sounded worried. "I'm sorry, but I thought I'd better let you know that Mr. Morgan is looking for you."

Alex wanted to swear. Neville Morgan, the senior partner Alex reported to, knew perfectly well that she was going out for a rare lunch with friends; she'd told him about it herself just the day before. Still, when a senior partner at the well-respected firm of Pence Whitfield snapped his fingers, mere junior associates jumped—and previous arrangements went down the drain.

"I'll be right there, Sharon," she said with resignation. She took two more bites of her crab salad, but the delicacy had lost its flavor. "Back to work," she announced. "Sorry, but things have been awfully busy lately."

"And a little edgy, I'll bet, with Kane Forrestal in exile," a blond-haired securities broker murmured.

"What do you mean, exile?" Alex asked. "He's on vacation."

The woman laughed. "Now that sounds like an official company line if ever I heard one. Pence Whitfield senior associates don't take vacations, Alex. The talk on the street is that he was fired."

Another young business executive chimed in. "I wouldn't be surprised if it's true. That last deal of his can't have made the partners at Pence Whitfield very happy. Losing his nerve like that..."

"It was a perfectly reasonable outcome for our client," Alex said stiffly.

"Backing down on a hostile takeover after all the strategy was in place?" The executive's voice was crisp. "Come on, Alex. You can't be that naive. Kane Forrestal is history. Of course, it leaves a nice opening for some younger associate."

"He's on vacation," Alex repeated.

But the words rang hollow in her mind as she made her way back through the skywalks to the new glass tower where Pence Whitfield, the biggest law firm in the Twin Cities, occupied three full floors. What was it the broker had said? "Pence Whitfield senior associates don't take vacations." Yes, that was it. And she was right, Alex thought. They certainly didn't disappear for weeks at a time as Kane Forrestal had....

Or as he seemed to have done, Alex reminded herself. A mere junior associate like herself wasn't in a position to know where Kane Forrestal was or what he might be doing. His specialty was mergers and acquisitions; he could be anywhere in the world quietly negotiating some new deal by now. It certainly was none of Alex's business. She'd worked with him on only one case, not long after she'd joined the firm—before she'd settled into the group of attorneys who worked almost exclusively with wills, estates and trusts. And she had talked to him on a few other occasions—once at a company Christmas party, and now and then at the coffee machine, in the halls or on the way to the parking garage.

That was the extent of her acquaintance with Kane Forrestal, so it was dead certain no one was going to make a point of letting Alex know what he was up to. In fact, it would be pretty conceited of her to think that someone should!

Sharon looked up from her computer terminal as Alex came in. "Mr. Morgan said to go right to his office when you got back. He didn't say what it was about, but he called a group meeting for lunch. Here's the agenda his secretary brought down."

"Damn," Alex muttered. "I told him yesterday I wouldn't be available."

"Did your friend like the crystal baby bottle?"

"Ah, yes. That's what you sent." Alex didn't look up from the single-spaced sheet. "She said she adored it. Thanks, Sharon. I'd be completely lost without you." Running a hand over her sleek French twist to be certain that each dark strand of hair was still in place, she headed off down the hall toward Neville Morgan's office.

Don't anticipate trouble, she told herself. *This summons will probably turn out to be nothing at all.* It certainly wasn't unusual for him to call an associate in alone to talk about a project.

As one of the eleven senior partners of Pence Whitfield, Neville Morgan had long occupied an enormous corner office, walnut-paneled and deeply carpeted—and so quiet that the view of downtown Minneapolis from the window behind his desk might have been a silent film projected on a blank wall.

The silver-haired lawyer was just putting down the telephone when his secretary sent Alex in.

"I'm sorry to have missed the meeting," she said. "If I'd known, I could have changed my plans."

"It wasn't critical for you to be here. Of course, I wouldn't like you to make a habit of missing group meetings. But that wasn't what I called you in to talk about." Neville Morgan leaned back with an expansive smile and waved a hand at a chair. "Alexandra, how would you like to spend a couple of weeks in Duluth?"

Duluth? Alex wondered how he would react if she told the truth and said, "Not at all, thank you. I'd rather have a root canal." She didn't have any particular prejudice against Duluth—she'd never been there—but what she did know about the place wasn't inviting. It was a small city, little more than an overgrown town, really. Because of its position at the western tip of Lake Superior, it was a shipping port for iron ore. And that, from everything Alex had ever heard, was about the biggest attraction it held.

But she knew perfectly well that, despite the phrasing of the question, she wasn't really being given a choice, so she sat down and folded her hands primly on her note-book. "Of course. What will I be doing?"

Neville Morgan smiled. The expression was almost feline, because his incisors were noticeably longer than the rest of his teeth. "I knew I could count on you, Alexandra." He interlaced his fingers across the expanse of his vest. "It involves an estate, of course. A long-term client of ours, Geoffrey Wintergreen, died recently, and since it's an extensive estate, the executor—his nephew, Paul—requires legal counsel. Also, I'm afraid one of the other heirs is making noises about overturning the will— hopes to increase his share. So in order to be certain that nothing is overlooked..."

Alex wanted to groan. She knew what was coming.

"You can plan on being up there a couple of weeks at least, just getting things set up properly and the preliminary papers filed. We'll have to decide how to handle the troublesome heir first. Of course, I'll be available for consultation at all times."

Alex nodded. This was standard procedure, part of the learning period—almost an apprenticeship—for every young attorney. The associates took care of the paperwork, the drudgery, the details. The senior partners supervised and added the finishing touches.

"And of course, if you get into any trouble," Neville Morgan added genially, "you can call on Kane for help."

Warning bells went off in Alex's head. It would never have occurred to her to consult Kane Forrestal about how to settle an estate. Without a doubt he could get through the paperwork necessary to probate a will, but Pence Whitfield attorneys were all specialists, and Kane's field was about as far from estates and trusts as it was possible to get. Had he been demoted? Or had he tired of mergers and acquisitions and asked for a transfer? Or...

"In fact," Neville Morgan continued, "that's an order, Alexandra."

She was silent for a moment, letting the implications of that statement sink in. Finally she said, "You're telling me to get myself into some kind of minor difficulty and call Kane?"

He waved a hand. "Minor, major. Doesn't matter. Just find an excuse to call him."

Alex shook her head in confusion. "Where on earth is he?"

"In Duluth. Where do you think?"

She frowned. "What's he doing there?"

"Living in a shack on the north shore of Lake Superior and not talking to anybody."

"I see," Alex said slowly. "But if he isn't talking..."

"It isn't that he *won't* talk, you understand. It's just that he doesn't make any sense when he does. For instance, he told my secretary he's going to be a beachcomber for a while."

"A beachcomber?" Her voice was slightly shrill with surprise. "He isn't...ill, is he?"

"You mean mentally? Hell, no," Neville Morgan scoffed. "I believe he wants us to think he's up there doing penance."

"Penance for what?"

"He blew this last deal—the Quadrangle takeover—and he wants us to think he's ashamed of himself. And he ought to be, to tell the truth. But we're reasonable people. There isn't a senior partner here who doesn't have the same sort of skeleton in his closet. We've all made bad deals from time to time, and Kane knows it. So I don't think he's up there licking his wounds. He's plotting something. I want you to go and find out what he really wants."

Alex doodled her name on the corner of her notebook. "I'm still not sure I understand."

"He says he doesn't know if he wants to come back to the firm at all."

"That's ridiculous."

"My point exactly. If he intended to resign, he'd have carried out the threat by now. But officially he's on vacation. I want to know what he's holding out for—so I can offer him the least possible to get him back where he belongs. There are deals hanging in the wind all over the world waiting for him."

Alex nibbled thoughtfully on her thumbnail. "Why me, Mr. Morgan? Wouldn't it be better to send someone who knows him better than I do?"

His eyebrows lifted. "What kind of negotiator are you, Alexandra? It wouldn't be very smart to send a senior partner up there first thing, would it? We'd give away all our bargaining strength if we let Kane feel indispensable."

Even if he is, Alex thought. That was what Neville Morgan was really saying.

"Besides, you're the one with the best excuse. There just aren't any public-finance deals, or tax problems, or big bankruptcies going on in Duluth just now, or we'd send those people."

Alex considered that and nodded. "What if he really *does* feel too ashamed to come back?"

Neville Morgan's chair creaked as he stood up. "Then you offer him our forgiveness, my dear. But I doubt we'll get off that cheaply."

It was apparent that he considered the interview over, but Alex stayed stubbornly in her chair. "If I'm going up to negotiate, you'd better tell me what you're prepared to offer him—otherwise there's no sense in my going. How far are you willing to go?''

''Quite a long way, actually. He wants a partnership? Fine. That's not far off, anyway, though you don't need to tell him that. Bigger office, another secretary, more money—''

''Even after the Quadrangle mess?''

''Everybody messes up once. Kane won't make the same mistake again, and next time he'll be a real tiger.'' He moved across to the door. ''Just between you and me and this desk, Alexandra, the senior partners are so anxious to get him back that Kane can have just about anything he wants. Anything within reason, of course. I'll get a memo to you this afternoon about the Wintergreen estate. My secretary has the case file.''

Alex nodded absently. For a moment she'd forgotten about the ostensible reason for her trip.

''Pull this off smoothly, and it will look very good on your record, my dear,'' Neville Morgan added. ''It will probably speed your own climb up the ladder, if you get my meaning.'' He patted her shoulder. ''Keep me posted, Alex. I'm counting on you.''

IT WAS ALMOST NINE that night before she left the office, but all the paperwork on her desk was cleaned up, and Neville Morgan's memo was tucked securely in her calfskin briefcase. She started to drive across Minneapolis toward the apartment complex where she lived, but halfway there she changed her mind and turned toward a lessdesirable neighborhood, the section of the city where she'd grown up. She parked her little car in the empty lot next to a small building that housed a restaurant and bar and went in.

Jacobi's hadn't changed one iota since her childhood, when Alex would come in after classes, empty her schoolbag, climb up on the end stool at the bar and do her homework under her father's watchful eye. It even smelled the same, Alex thought, with the sharp spicy aroma of smoked pork and sauerkraut wafting from the kitchen to mix with the pungent scent of beer from the kegs.

Behind the carved-oak bar, a big man with pewter-gray hair and a bushy mustache stopped polishing a glass and looked Alex over from the top of her sleek French twist to the toes of her Italian pumps. For a moment she half expected him to bark, "Where are your books, young lady?"

Instead, Gus Jacobi said critically, "You're looking a little peaked."

"I stayed to work late, Papa." She climbed onto a bar stool.

Gus appeared to think that over, then shook his head. "Long hours never hurt anyone. But not eating, now, that hurts. Don't suppose you'd turn down a little sauerbraten." He didn't wait for an answer, just pushed open the swinging door to the kitchen and called, "Fix up a nice plate for my Alex, will you?"

Alex smiled. That, too, was an echo from her schooldays. It was a wonder she hadn't been a blimp. Oh, well, she told herself, she *was* hungry, and Jacobi's served the best sauerbraten in the Twin Cities.

Gus selected a thick bar glass and filled it from a tap behind the bar. "Here," he said as he pushed the foaming brew across to her.

"Not on an empty stomach, Papa."

"Drink it. Beer's good for you. All kinds of vitamins. Builds up your blood, too." He went back to polishing glasses. "What brings you out here in the middle of the week, anyway?"

"I have to make a business trip. I'm leaving tomorrow and I won't be back for a couple of weeks at least."

"Where to this time?"

"Duluth."

One of the waiters appeared with a platter piled high with food. It looked, Alex thought, as if the chef had simply ladled on an ample helping of every dish the kitchen could produce. She opened the napkin-wrapped bundle he handed her and picked up her fork.

Gus grunted. "Duluth? Is that the best your fancy-schmantzy bunch of lawyers can do? How come you never get to New York? Or Paris? Or Tokyo?"

"People in Duluth have legal problems, too, Papa. And this is an important job. It's going to take a lot of tact and diplomacy, and if I pull it off, it means I've got the quality senior partners look for. Mr. Morgan as good as said it's a big step toward my being made a partner."

His eyes narrowed. "Does that mean he's going to Duluth with you?"

Alex chewed a bite of schnitzel and counted to ten. "No, he's not. And if you mean, did he suggest that the best way to a partnership is to sleep with him—no, he didn't. That kind of thing is not only unethical, it's illegal, Papa."

"Lots of things are illegal," Gus said cynically. "Doesn't mean they don't go on."

Her patience slipped a little more. "Why don't you let me worry about that? I'm the attorney."

"I'm not likely to forget it. Who put you through law school, anyway? Just you mind my words, girl. Don't you let them tuck you away somewhere invisible where they can forget about you. Duluth!" He sniffed.

"They won't, Papa. Believe me." She pushed buttered noodles around on her plate. "George sends his best, by the way."

Gus sniffed again. "Tell him if he gets tired of being a fancy maître d', he can always come back where he belongs."

Alex smiled. "I'll certainly tell him." She sipped her beer. *Perhaps I have a future in labor negotiations,* she thought. *I've picked up two cases in one day....*

A middle-aged man came in; Gus drew another picture-perfect mug of beer, slid it down the bar to the customer and asked him, "Have you met my daughter, the high-powered lawyer?"

Alex nodded politely to the customer. Gus had always been this way, she reflected, ever since her mother had died of cancer and left him with a ten-year-old to raise. He scolded and corrected Alex at every opportunity, but burst his buttons with pride whenever he mentioned her to someone else.

"That reminds me," Gus said. "I've handed out all your business cards, Alex."

She fished a dozen out of her handbag and handed them over. She'd long ago given up the idea of convincing her father that Pence Whitfield was not likely to pick up a lot of business from Jacobi's clientele.

Gus glanced at the card, a classic off-white vellum with raised black lettering. "Not very flashy, is it?" he observed. "You'd think maybe they'd put your picture on it or something." He polished another glass to a gleam and set it on a shelf behind the bar. "I found that hoop thing of your mother's you wanted. It's on her dressing table upstairs."

"The quilting hoop? Thanks, Papa, but—" Alex bit her tongue. She had asked for the hoop months ago, when she still had hopes of completing the quilt for Joanna's baby. Gus had veered away from the subject, as if after all these years he still hadn't been able to face going through his wife's belongings, and so Alex had let the matter drop.

Now that he'd brought himself to search for the hoop, Alex couldn't throw his effort back in his face. "Thanks, Papa," she said softly, and reached across the bar to pat his cheek. "I'll run up and get it. Then I'd better go home and get some sleep so I can be on the road early."

"Duluth," he said once more, sounding disgusted. She smiled at him from the door, and he called, "Don't forget to eat!"

ONCE ALEX WAS OUT OF Minneapolis, there was no missing the road. It was a monotonous ribbon of concrete, punctuated now and then by a town, a forest of deep green pine or a stunning view of one of Minnesota's ten thousand lakes. In fact, the highway was so easy to follow that she let her mind drift ahead to Duluth and the two tasks that awaited her there.

From Neville Morgan's memo, it was apparent that Geoffrey Wintergreen's estate might be a major headache even without a squabble over the will. It was certainly not just a textbook exercise engineered as an excuse to get her to Duluth.

But that sort of problem, while not exactly commonplace, was precisely the kind of challenge Alex had become expert at sorting out in her three years with Pence Whitfield. The question of Kane Forrestal was something else altogether.

"They're sending an amateur to negotiate with a man who's put together international economic deals," she muttered. "It's insane, when you think about it."

And that kind of negative thinking was going to get her nowhere, she reminded herself. Instead, she focused on the fact that Neville Morgan had obviously thought she could pull the job off, or he wouldn't have sent her. And if she did succeed, he'd practically promised her a partnership not too far in the future. Maybe even before she was thirty, and that was only three years away....

Alex spotted a sign marking the city limits of Duluth just as the little car topped a hill and started down a long grade into the worst pea-soup fog she'd ever seen. She could hardly see two car lengths ahead. Street signs were a lost cause; by the time she caught a glimpse of one, she was past it. She was afraid to slow down to a crawl for fear someone behind her, more familiar with the terrain, would be moving too fast to stop.

In the end she drove around town for nearly an hour before she finally stumbled across the street she was looking for and found the bed-and-breakfast where her secretary had reserved a room for her.

When Sharon had recommended the place, Alex had expressed doubts; she needed privacy so she could work, not a hostess who wanted to chat over coffee for hours with a newfound friend. And how could a busy attorney function without room service or at least a restaurant on the premises? But Sharon had said this was more of an inn than a private home, and if she was going to spend two weeks, maybe more, there, she might as well be comfortable.

Alex's first glimpse of the place convinced her that it would certainly be an experience to remember. The bed-and-breakfast wasn't an ordinary house at all, but a brick Federal-style mansion, nestled in a grove of pine trees at a discreet distance from the street. In the fog, the house had an almost ghostly quality—but any spirits present were nice ones, Alex thought. Nothing threatening at all.

She signed the register and let the bellboy carry her two-suiter and laptop computer up to her room. Sharon hadn't spared Pence Whitfield's expense account; Alex's room had obviously once been the master suite, with an enormous bath and an attached sitting room. Alex looked around at the comfortable overstuffed furniture, the desk, the canopy bed, and sighed in satisfaction. Then she asked the bellboy to bring her a pot of tea, and she sat down to make her first telephone call while she waited.

The call was not to Paul Wintergreen, Geoffrey's nephew and executor, but to Kane Forrestal. She might as well get started right away, she reasoned.

After seven rings Alex broke the connection. "Great," she muttered. "I forgot to ask Mr. Morgan exactly how I'm supposed to talk to the man if he doesn't answer his phone." She eyed the address Neville Morgan had given her. Then she remembered the fog and concluded that if she went out in it again she might be lost for days.

And why, she suddenly wondered, would anyone who didn't *have* to go anywhere be out in this kind of weather? In pure annoyance, she dialed Kane Forrestal's number again, and this time she let it ring. Ten, twenty, twenty-five—

There was a click and a moment's hesitation before a deep voice said, "Forrestal."

Alex had always thought that Kane Forrestal's voice was one of his greatest assets. It was as soft and deep and pure and rich as velvet. At the moment, however, it had a rough edge. In fact, he sounded as if he'd been asleep.

Alex glanced at her watch. No, she decided. She was not going to apologize to the man even if she had awakened him; it was one o'clock in the afternoon.

"Mr. Forrestal, this is Alexandra Jacobi. I'm calling because—"

His voice warmed into amusement. "What can't Pence Whitfield live without today?"

Alex bit her lip and said cautiously, "I don't understand what you mean, I'm afraid. I'm in Duluth to do some work on an estate, and Neville Morgan suggested . . ."

In the background she could hear the murmur of a woman's voice. Alex thought she heard, "Shall I go, Kane?"

He didn't bother to muffle the telephone. "Of course not. This isn't important."

Something at his end of the line creaked. Probably a bedspring, Alex thought disgustedly. All right, so he hadn't been asleep, after all. At least now she knew why it had taken two tries and twenty-five rings to get an answer.

She went on coolly, "He suggested I might want to get in touch with you to see if you knew the family. The client's name—"

"Why on earth should I know who he is? Or was?"

Alex blinked. "Well, since you're living here, I assumed—"

"Attorneys should never assume anything, Miss Jacobi. Didn't Neville tell you I'm a hermit now?"

She shifted her grip on the receiver. "Mr. Forrestal, I really would like your advice on how to deal with this problem."

His yawn was unmistakable. "I can't see why. You're a perfectly competent attorney."

"I'm very flattered, Mr. Forrestal, but—"

"Oh, it's nothing personal. And it's no real compliment, either. Pence Whitfield wouldn't have hired you if you weren't competent. So you go out there and do your stuff, Miss Jacobi. I'm sure you'll be just fine."

And the dull buzz of a severed connection sounded in her ear.

CHAPTER TWO

ALEX GRITTED HER TEETH and replaced the receiver very gently rather than slamming it down as she'd have liked to. Damn the man, anyway! she thought. He could at least have listened.

And as for that crack about her competence—it was obvious Kane Forrestal didn't really even remember her. Three years ago, when she'd been assigned to help his team with the Sullivan case, he'd seemed to appreciate her work. In fact, he'd told her at the time that she'd done a good job. True, the comment had been almost brusque, but it was more recognition than the rest of the team had gotten. For him to say now that he knew she was competent only because she was on the payroll, when it was apparent that he'd recalled her name and not much more, was insulting.

This is not a professional attitude, Alex admonished herself. *You simply cannot allow yourself to take his remarks personally. You have a job to do.*

She took six slow deep breaths, a stress-relieving trick she'd learned in law school. Then she called her client, only to be told by his secretary that Paul Wintergreen was too busy to see her that afternoon.

It was annoying, but not unexpected. Keeping an attorney waiting for an extra day would hardly cause a flicker in the man's bank balance, considering the size of the inheritance he was about to come into. In the meantime it would give her a chance to work on Kane Forrestal—assuming she could think of another approach.

Alex's pot of tea arrived on a silver tray lined with a real lace doily and carried by a plump white-haired woman in an old-fashioned floral-print housedress. "I'm Mrs. Keith, the head housekeeper," she said. "If there's anything special you'd like during your stay, I hope you'll let me know. We do try to pamper our visitors here at the Guest House."

"Do you have a fax machine?" Alex asked.

Mrs. Keith didn't even blink. "Of course. We can install one right here in your room if you like." She glanced across at the draperies, which were stirring gently. "Goodness, dear, you look as if you're freezing. Didn't the bellboy offer to close the windows?"

Alex hadn't realized she had goose bumps. Was it the chilly air, or was it the cold shoulder she'd gotten from Kane Forrestal? "I don't think I gave him a chance to offer," she said. "I was too anxious for my tea."

Mrs. Keith bustled across to close the casements. "The air from the lake is so damp when it gets foggy that it seems to cut right through the skin."

"Are we close to the lake?" Alex moved across to the window, but all she could see was shifting fog.

"Close enough that the water moderates the temperatures all year round."

Alex shivered. "This is moderate? It's the middle of summer!"

Mrs. Keith smiled. "You don't know the city very well, do you?"

"Not at all." Alex reached into her briefcase for the slip of paper with Kane Forrestal's address. "Can you give me directions?"

"Of course." Mrs. Keith perched a pair of Ben Franklin spectacles on her nose and studied the address. "Oh, this is easy."

"Don't overestimate me," Alex muttered.

"Then I'll write it down, just in case."

After the housekeeper had gone, Alex slowly drank her tea and flipped through the Wintergreen file. But even as she stared at the draft copy of Geoffrey Wintergreen's will and the newspaper clippings about his life and death, she wasn't thinking of the estate.

Another telephone call to Kane Forrestal would probably get her no further than the last one had—if he answered the telephone at all this time. Bearding the lion in his den would be equally risky, but what choice did she have? She had to establish direct contact somehow; she couldn't negotiate with a shadow. Surely he wouldn't slam the door on her—would he?

She closed the file with a thump and reached for her car keys.

The fog seemed even thicker as she drove, and for a while Alex thought she'd missed the edge of the city altogether and was well on her way to Canada. But once she spotted the first of the landmarks Mrs. Keith had noted, she had no trouble finding her way.

However, the address did not come close to matching Neville Morgan's description of Kane Forrestal's new home. "A shack," he'd said. But though the house that bore the number on Alex's slip of paper could not by any stretch of the imagination be called a mansion, it wasn't exactly built of tar paper, either.

It was a neat, sturdy, unpretentious story-and-a-half house, stained a dark grayish brown that seemed to melt into the landscape. The mailbox by the road sported a sign that read, "Inglenook." There were curtains at the windows and a stack of firewood at the corner of the house. It looked like a well-established home, not a place someone had just moved into temporarily.

Alex checked the address again. The number was right, and in the drive was a fire-engine-red Ferrari. The license plate on the back of it read, "I DEAL."

This was the place, all right, Alex told herself. And Neville Morgan was right about Kane Forrestal, too. Anyone who drove a car like that one and had the arrogance to put such a boast on the plates, wasn't going to be content with beachcombing for long.

She left her car barricading the drive and crossed the deck to the nearest door, at the side of the house. But there'd been no need to block his escape route; if Kane Forrestal was there, he apparently didn't want company, for no one answered the bell.

Just in case it wasn't working, Alex hammered on the door, stopping only when her fist began to ache.

There was a rustle behind her, and Alex wheeled around to see a middle-aged woman with her arms propped on top of the fence next door. "He's not home," the woman said helpfully.

"His car is here."

"He left on a bicycle."

"That figures." Alex frowned. "Are you expecting him back soon?"

"Can't say. Maybe. He comes and goes a lot."

"I'm not surprised." Alex fished a business card out of her bag and leaned against the side of the house while she debated what sort of message to leave. Finally she wrote, "As a professional courtesy to a colleague, will you please call me? I'm staying at the Guest House, and I'm interested in any insight you might have on my case."

She stuck the card into the crack of the door and dusted off her hands.

The appeal to professional courtesy might work, she thought. The longer an attorney practiced, the more it became almost automatic to grant a favor asked by the opposition, because next week the home team might need one in return. By now, professional courtesy must be a way of life for Kane Forrestal.

She drove back to the Guest House and spent the rest of the afternoon studying Geoffrey Wintergreen's will. It was plainly Neville Morgan's work; his turn of phrase jumped out at her from every convoluted paragraph.

Kane Forrestal didn't call.

Alex asked Mrs. Keith to bring her dinner upstairs and decided to take a bath while she waited. As she soaked in a luxuriously deep tub, she considered her next move. For all she knew, the man might have simply shredded her card and tossed it into the trash.

Don't give up yet, she told herself. She didn't know for sure that he wouldn't talk to her; perhaps he wasn't home yet.

Then she jeered at herself. What did she expect him to be doing? Still riding his bicycle in the fog?

All right, she reflected. Maybe he was just holding out a bit till she was good and worried, and he'd turn up in a day or two. She should just sit tight and pretend that it didn't matter, and perhaps he'd be the one to start questioning *her.*

Or perhaps he intended to negotiate from a position of strength, and he wouldn't talk to a lowly associate as long as there was a chance of getting a senior partner to come up for a chat. The man was an expert at this sort of thing. He could certainly keep the pressure on longer than Alex could.

And if that happened, sooner or later she was going to have to face Neville Morgan and tell him she hadn't even gotten to first base with Kane Forrestal.

Well, she thought with resignation, there was still the Wintergreen estate to be settled, so she wouldn't be sitting around doing nothing while she waited. And if she could finesse the Wintergreen job, at least the damage might be mitigated....

"What a quitter!" she told herself in disgust. "You're ready to give up before you've even started!"

Still, she had to admit that the half-promised partnership was looking more and more like a wistful dream.

Alex didn't realize that she'd lost track of time until she heard a knock on her sitting-room door. Here was Mrs. Keith with her dinner, and Alex was still lying in a rapidly cooling tub daydreaming.

"Just a minute," she called. "I'm sorry, Mrs. Keith. I'll be right there!"

A dark green plush terry robe, courtesy of the Guest House, was hanging on the back of the bathroom door. Alex scrambled into it, piled her hair into a dripping wad and wrapped a towel around it turban-style, then pushed her feet into a pair of satin mules. When she pulled the hall door open, her turban slipped, and as she bent her head to catch it, she said, "I'd like it over there on the table, please."

There was no answer, and no movement from the door to the suite.

Alex pushed the towel out of her eyes. In the very spot where she'd expected to see Mrs. Keith's soft smile was a distinctly masculine chest.

She closed her eyes in pain. When she opened them again, the chest was still there, but a pair of arms was crossed over it. She looked up into Kane Forrestal's face.

Strictly speaking, his looks were distinguished rather than handsome. His chiseled face was one any sculptor would have been proud to claim, with its determined chin, strong nose and interesting hollows under the cheekbones. At the moment his wide-set dark gray eyes held an expression of slight bemusement.

"On the table?" Kane Forrestal said gently. "Well...if you insist, though frankly it seems a bit kinky to me. Is *that* what you meant when you asked for professional courtesy?"

Color flooded Alex's face, a reaction that took her by surprise. She'd worked so long and hard at getting that response under control that she'd have sworn nothing could embarrass her anymore.

"I was addressing Mrs. Keith about where to put my dinner," she said repressively. "And you're obviously not her."

"No. Obviously not," he parroted. He sounded solemn, but there was a wicked gleam in his eye. "I do beg your pardon, Miss Jacobi. But you really should be more careful about what you say if you don't want to be misunderstood."

"Would you please get out of here?" Alex snapped. "I don't intend to stand here and discuss it while I drip all over the floor." She instantly thought better of trying to throw him out. What if he actually went away?

She tried again. "Just give me a minute to get out of this bathrobe."

His mouth quirked in amusement.

Alex supposed he was going to take that as an invitation, too. "I mean . . ."

The amusement grew into a rich deep chuckle, and the corners of his eyes crinkled very nicely. "Will it ease your

mind if I wait downstairs while you pull yourself together, Miss Jacobi?''

''That would be very kind of you,'' Alex said stiffly.

''And don't worry about me changing my mind and
vanishing. You're far too... amusing to walk out on.''

She closed the door and, leaning against it, muttered
under her breath, ''Forrestal one, Jacobi nothing.''
Dammit, he'd already managed to put her on the defensive, and with such a timeworn trick, too—sexist comments.

She pushed herself away from the door. He must think
she was an extraordinarily easy mark. Well, he'd soon see
that she wasn't; he wouldn't get that reaction again.
She'd show him that sexual innuendo didn't ruffle her.

By the time Alex descended the stairs a few minutes
later, she had regained her poise. At least he was here, she
reminded herself. She'd have a chance to make her point,
and no matter what he said, she wouldn't have to go back
to Minneapolis in *complete* ignominy.

She spotted him, sitting in a leather wing chair in the
great entrance hall, apparently studying the pattern of the
stained glass in the front door. The subdued light cut his
face into acute angles and cast a silvery gleam onto his
dark hair, making her think of how he might look in
thirty years. The elder statesman of the conference room,
she thought. Or the kind of lawyer who could stir a
courtroom just by showing up.

He came to meet her at the foot of the wide staircase.
Alex could have sworn she saw the barest flicker of appreciation in his eyes as he took in her dress—a jade-
green sleeveless jersey knit that skimmed her slender figure perfectly, making her look sophisticated, but very
much a woman.

He probably assumed I'd come down in the least-feminine thing I own, she thought. She was glad she hadn't fallen into that trap. What a mistake it would have been to let Kane Forrestal know his remarks had affected her in the slightest. It was important to let him know she was comfortable with her femininity.

But the expression in his eyes was so fleeting it was impossible to know for sure if she'd actually seen it. And all he said was, "You seemed to be expecting dinner, so I—"

"It doesn't matter." *Seemed to be,* she thought irritably. Was he implying that perhaps she'd been making a pass at him, after all?

"But it does matter," he said earnestly. "I wouldn't like to be responsible for letting you go hungry, so I took the liberty of reserving a table for us in the dining room."

Alex had the feeling he expected an objection, so she said calmly, "That's very good thinking, Mr. Forrestal."

"Oh, call me Kane. Don't you think professional courtesy allows that, Alexandra?" His voice was low and almost husky.

A bedroom whisper, she thought, no doubt intended to send a tingle along her nerves. Well, it had done that, all right, but it was a tingle of disappointment in his tactics, not at all the sort Kane had in mind, she was sure.

She gave him a bright and meaningless smile. "It's Alex, please." She turned toward the dining room, through an arched doorway draped with heavy velvet.

The big room held a good number of tables, and most were occupied. Mrs. Keith showed them to a table for two by the fireplace. Alex asked for a sherry.

Kane ordered a scotch-and-water and said, "I almost didn't find your card, you know. When I opened the door, it went fluttering down into a crack between the house and the deck. Took me the rest of the afternoon to fish it out.''

Alex allowed the barest hint of irony to creep into her voice. "How conscientious of you."

"Oh, I had to go after it. It might have been something that really mattered," Kane assured her. "Why didn't you just put it inside on the kitchen table?"

"You mean the door was unlocked?"

"Of course."

"And why not?" Alex murmured. "You have a very efficient watchdog right next door."

"Eleanor? Yes, she's quite attentive." He paused. "So, what can I do for you, Alex? In the name of professional courtesy, of course."

The waiter brought their drinks. Alex toyed with her glass and tried to fight down the warmth that insisted on rising into her cheeks. "The first thing you can do, Kane, is cut out the suggestive remarks. They aren't going to get you anywhere." Her tone was almost chiding, like a parent to a child. "In any case, I don't think you can actually enjoy them. You're far too professional to behave like that."

His eyebrows arched a little.

"Just treat me as you would any male colleague, and we'll get along fine." She almost reached across the table to pat his arm in reassurance, but decided that would be going a little too far. She sipped her sherry, instead, and changed the subject. "I'm working on the Wintergreen estate."

"Wintergreen?"

His bland tone annoyed her. "If you've read a newspaper at all while you've been in Duluth, Kane, you must have heard that Geoffrey Wintergreen is dead. It seems to have been the biggest news of the month.''

''Oh, yes. I heard. Are you working for Paul Playboy or the other side?''

She let the nickname pass and focused on the important issue. ''Then it's not just talk? Ralph Wintergreen's threat to have the will overturned, I mean?''

Kane shrugged. ''I wouldn't know, of course. But the way I hear it, Ralph thinks he was promised a whole lot more than the will actually gave him, and he's not happy about cousin Paul's getting the balance.'' He moved an ice cube around his drink with the tip of his index finger. Then he shook his head and smiled slightly.

''What's so amusing?''

''That you really are working on the Wintergreen matter.''

Alex looked at him steadily. ''Why shouldn't I be?''

''I thought for a while this afternoon that you were anxious to get in touch because Pence Whitfield sent you up here to make a deal with me.''

She blinked in what she hoped looked like innocent confusion. ''Make a deal over what?''

He waggled a finger at her. ''Don't play dumb, Alex. Everybody in the firm must know by now that I'm hiding out up here.''

She let her gaze drop to the spotless white tablecloth. ''There's been some talk, of course,'' she admitted. ''I've been too busy to pay much attention.''

''Well, I'm glad to know you're not involved in any hijinks.''

The waiter reappeared with their appetizers. Alex was glad of the excuse to study her plate; she recognized chunks of tomatoes and mushrooms, though most of the ingredients were a mystery to her.

But the unfamiliar appetizer was not the source of the little flutter in the pit of her stomach. She tried to reason it away. She'd certainly not lied to him, and there was no reason whatever for her to feel disloyal just because she hadn't spilled out the whole truth.

"So why are you hiding out?" she asked. She cautiously nibbled a piece of mushroom. It had a delicate spicy flavor she'd never tasted before. "If you don't mind telling me, of course."

He stabbed a tomato chunk and stared at it. "Because I figured three-quarters of a million miles on my frequent-flier plans were enough."

His tone was almost flippant, which confirmed to Alex that he had no intention of carrying out his threats to leave the firm. But she decided to play along for the moment. "And so you're going to be a beachcomber in Duluth."

"Right." He rewarded her with a smile.

"Why Duluth, anyway? Why not Florida or Hawaii?"

He snorted. "Too many people. I like Lake Superior. It's quiet and peaceful—not as many tourists find their way up here."

"How do you plan to pay your bills?" She couldn't remember at the moment, if indeed she'd ever known, whether he had family money to draw on. "You have to pay the rent on your little cottage somehow."

"If I run out of money, I might just set myself up as a wholesale supplier of driftwood."

She had to swallow hard before she could say, "There's a market for that sort of thing?"

"Of course. And there's an endless supply to choose from on the beach, and with the prices they want for it in some stores in the Twin Cities, I could get rich."

Alex didn't quite trust herself to comment. He sounded serious, but of course that didn't mean he was telling the truth. Still, even if she looked at it as an opening gambit in a negotiation—where grandstand gestures were commonplace—the idea of Kane Forrestal's peddling driftwood was too bizarre for belief.

The waiter reappeared with the veal Alex had ordered earlier and some sort of fish for Kane. It wasn't the fish's fault that Alex didn't recognize what kind it was, because all of it was there on the plate—head, fins and tail. She averted her eyes from the sight and said, "The name on your mailbox—what is it? Inglenook? Is that the owner?"

He shook his head. "It's the house's name."

"What does it mean?"

"Don't you know? An inglenook is a snug little corner by a fire. Which, if you think about it, is a pretty comforting place to be when the lake kicks up in a storm."

Alex frowned. "Mrs. Keith told me the water has a moderating influence on the weather."

"Oh, it does," Kane assured her. "It's always warmer near the shore in the winter than it is inland, and cooler in the summer, because the water acts like a gigantic geothermal reserve."

"I haven't any idea what you're talking about."

"The lake stores heat all summer and releases it slowly in the winter. And the breeze coming off the water in the summer is cooler than the surrounding air."

Alex remembered the breeze blowing in through the window of her room and shivered.

"So we have natural heating and air-conditioning. And it's free, courtesy of the largest fresh body of water in the world. Around here, we call it the lake effect."

She savored a perfectly cooked baby carrot and said, "I can see why you'd appreciate the results. You wouldn't have to pick up as much driftwood to pay your utility bills."

He smiled approvingly. "Exactly."

"I'm not sure I agree it's so wonderful, though. It's the middle of August, and frankly, if there was a log in that fireplace I'd set a match to it."

"Of course, you're not exactly dressed for Duluth," he said, eyeing her bare arms with slow appreciation. "Not that your dress is unattractive, by any means, just not quite suited to the climate."

I asked for that one, Alex told herself.

"You also have to understand that summer only sticks around up here for about twelve days."

"What do you plan to do the rest of the time? You certainly can't beachcomb in the winter."

Kane shrugged. "I haven't thought about it. Maybe I'll take up chain-saw sculpture."

I'll bet, Alex thought. The truth was probably that he hadn't thought about it because he intended to be back in the thick of things long before winter came. Now if she could only find out what it was going to take to get him home where he belonged....

She shook her head. "I don't understand you, Kane. It's hard to believe you could turn your back on a career you obviously love, and one you're so very good at."

"What a lovely thing to say, Alex."

She tried again. "Isn't there anything that would make you stay in law?"

"Can't think of a thing."

She smothered a sigh. She was getting nowhere fast. If she started naming some options, not only would her own cover be blown, but she might simply put ideas into his head—things he wouldn't have asked for on his own.

The waiter cleared away their plates and said, "We have a lovely dessert cart tonight. There's a seven-layer chocolate torte and—"

"Say no more," Kane ordered. "Bring it out." He shot a glance at Alex. "Especially since I'm not paying the bill."

She smiled ruefully. "I'm glad you're taking my instructions to heart about treating me as you would any male colleague."

"Oh, that's not it at all. But you're obviously on an expense account, so I figured I may as well have one more good meal on Pence Whitfield."

Alex chose fresh fruit from the cart, and the waiter served a medley of strawberries, blueberries and melon in a stemmed crystal dish. As she nibbled at her first strawberry she suddenly realized why Kane sounded so pleased with himself, and all the enjoyment went out of the luscious berry.

You fool, she told herself. *You're being used.*

Kane Forrestal was an expert at seeing through hidden motives. The Wintergreen estate might have been a good cover, but he could not have missed the obvious. He had to know that Alex had been sent to Duluth mainly to deal with him. And therefore he also knew that everything he said to Alex would go straight back to Neville Morgan and the other senior partners.

He's going to use me as a pipeline to the other side, Alex thought. *He's going to feed me all the propaganda he wants them to hear.* It would be just like feeding disinformation to the enemy's spy.

And Alex had almost fallen into the trap. That should have come as no surprise, actually; Kane was a cham-

pion at this sort of thrust-and-parry bargaining. Trying
to deal with him under these conditions—the ones he'd
maneuvered her into—was like trying to fence in a dark
room with an opponent who was wearing night-vision
goggles.

But how could she get things back on an even keel?
Better yet, how could she manage to push Kane off balance?

Kane was going into rapturous detail about the glories
of the seven-layer chocolate torte he'd chosen and telling
her how much she was missing by confining herself to
mere fruit.

The answer to her dilemma hit her, and Alex interrupted ruthlessly. "All right," she said. "We're treating
this as if we're on opposite sides in a war, and it's time to
stop. This is not the sort of problem where battling it out
as opponents will do either of us any good."

Kane paused with a forkful of chocolate, cherry filling and whipped cream balanced precariously in midair.

"We'll get a lot further if we put all the cards on the
table and just talk," Alex persisted. "So tell me. What do
you want from Pence Whitfield, Kane?"

Kane gave her a long look that reminded her of a basset hound in pain. "Do you mean you were lying to me
when you said you weren't here to deal?"

Alex wasn't fooled by the mournful note in his voice.
"Come off it, Kane. I wasn't lying any more than you
were about the driftwood business." He wouldn't look
her quite in the eye. Satisfied, Alex pressed her advantage. "You do understand, don't you, that I can't make
promises? But I am authorized to take any proposal at all
back to the partners."

He set the fork down and complained, "I think I liked
you better when you were dripping wet."

"I'll pretend I didn't hear that." She signaled the waiter for another cup of coffee and leaned forward, arms folded on the edge of the table. "Now let's get down to some serious negotiation."

"But I don't want anything, Alexandra."

"I don't believe you."

He cut another bite from his dessert and studied it thoughtfully. "Except perhaps another slice of this torte in a doggie bag to take home for tomorrow," he mused. "I probably wouldn't say no to that. But as far as Pence Whitfield goes, I wouldn't know where to begin."

CHAPTER THREE

THAT WAS ABSOLUTELY all Kane would say.

Not that Alex was foolish enough to push the issue; she didn't even object when he changed the subject. But she knew she'd hit a nerve when he started talking about the show that had just opened at the Minneapolis Institute of the Arts. If he really was so happy beachcombing in Duluth, why had he been in the Twin Cities admiring art? She suspected that if she hadn't upset his train of thought, he'd never have admitted being there at all.

So she drank her coffee quietly, putting in a comment here and there and smiling to herself. He knew where she stood now, and once he had a chance to think it through, he'd quickly realize that his best bet was to tell her exactly what he wanted and get the process under way. He certainly didn't have anything to gain by holding out for a talk with someone more senior; he could only lose by delaying.

And once he concluded that Alex was on the level and would be absolutely fair, he would deal. She was certain of it.

She was proud of herself for recognizing that the basic problem had been the way they were sparring like two boxers in a ring, when the truth was that they were in the same corner. Perhaps they preferred different means to the end, but the goal was the same. And now that they were back on the same team, they could work together toward a compromise solution.

Perhaps I do have a gift for negotiation, Alex thought.

They sat over coffee for another half hour, talking of art and dance and theater, and then she said good-night to him at the main door. "Think it over," she suggested. "And whenever you're ready to talk, I'll be around."

Kane's eyes gleamed. "I'm sure you will. The Wintergreen estate will take a while to sort out."

Mrs. Keith bustled by at that moment, and Alex acknowledged her with a nod. Then she smiled and offered Kane her hand. She wouldn't have been surprised if he'd raised it to his lips in some pseudocourtly gesture—another trick of one-upmanship. But he did not; he merely held her hand for a moment, his grip warm and firm, and then he walked out the door. The remaining wisps of fog swirled around him, turning him into a figure of mystery.

All he needed, she thought, was a deer-stalker hat and a pipe....

Alex floated dreamily up to her room. If it hadn't been so late, she'd have been tempted to call Neville Morgan and give him a progress report. He'd be pleased at what she'd managed to accomplish already.

But her reason for her sense of well-being went even deeper than that. She had held her own tonight in a give-and-take with a master of the form. Alex had always preferred the quieter end of the law. She was quite willing to let others enjoy the dramatic moments in a courtroom or at a tense bargaining table; she was far more content in her office, where she had time to think through a problem before committing herself to action. She'd always been competent when called on for snap judgments or quick arguments—there was never any question of that, or she wouldn't have made it through the demanding curriculum of law school. But she'd never been quite comfortable with working that way, and she'd always given a little sigh of relief when she was done.

But tonight she had positively enjoyed herself.

Perhaps, she thought, she had acted a bit hastily two years ago when she'd settled into the team that concentrated on estates and wills and trusts. The subject and the atmosphere had seemed to suit her perfectly at the time. But had she underestimated her potential? Had she settled for what was easiest and turned her back on challenge, rather than take the risks involved in trying out a whole new kind of thinking?

Perhaps, she thought, once Kane was back at Pence Whitfield where he belonged, she might ask him if he thought she had the right stuff to be on his team. She didn't pretend to understand all the twists and turns in the kind of negotiating he did all the time, but she was certainly intelligent enough to learn the techniques. His encouraging her to take up the challenge depended, really, on whether or not he thought she had potential. If he did, he might agree to be her mentor, to teach her all the things she would need to know....

Mrs. Keith was busy turning down the thick comforter on the canopied bed when Alex reached her suite. "I'll be out of here in a jiff," she said. "I intended to be finished before you came upstairs."

"Take your time," Alex said absently. "It's nice to be fussed over. I'm sorry about the last-minute change to my dinner plans, by the way. I wasn't expecting Mr. Forrestal tonight."

Mrs. Keith patted the pillows smooth. "Don't give it a second thought."

The tone of her voice was almost like a wink, Alex thought. *I'll bet she expected me to take my time saying good-night to him, too—and was very disappointed by the handshake!*

Why was it that so many people didn't believe that men and women could work together without sex getting in the way? Even Kane had given in to that old way of thinking tonight, with his double-meaning remarks.

No, Alex reminded herself, he hadn't "given in," he'd done it on purpose, using the opportunity to try to keep her off-balance. It had almost worked, too.

Mrs. Keith took a stack of fresh towels into the bathroom and returned with the used ones. "There," she said with satisfaction. "You sleep well, now, and if you're not warm enough, there's another blanket in that bottom drawer."

She'd probably stay and tuck me in and read me a story if I asked, Alex thought, and smiled. Yes, she could get used to being coddled.

She wandered over to the window and pulled the curtain back a bit. The fog was less dense now, and she could see the black cold mass of the lake through the shifting streaks of mist. It seemed to go on forever, but that must simply have been a trick of the weather. Surely she should have been able to see the other side from here.

She let the curtain fall back into place. With a yawn she removed her dress, stepped out of the matching high heels and flexed her feet in relief. She put on a dark-green satin nightshirt and sat down to brush her hair to a blue-black gleam. No matter how tired she was, Alex could never get to sleep until her hair was smooth and silky; she supposed it was because the action brought back one of the few real memories she had of her mother. Hannah Jacobi had faithfully brushed Alex's hair every evening while they talked about the day, and then braided it to keep it from tangling in the night...

Alex yawned and, putting the brush down, went to lay out her clothes for the next day. She had to move the unfinished baby quilt out of her way to dig into the bottom of her suitcase, and she sighed at her own idiocy in bringing the silly thing along. She had picked it up on a whim this morning on her way out of her apartment, mostly because the quilting hoop was still in the back of her car where she'd tossed it on leaving her father's restaurant last night.

"Whatever made me think I'd have time to sit in a corner and sew a fine seam?" she asked herself as she turned out the lights. Even the settling-down sounds of an unfamiliar house did not keep her awake for long.

She was just finishing her breakfast the next morning when the young man from the reception desk came into the dining room. "Miss Jacobi? There's a telephone call for you."

Alex snatched a last sip of coffee and put down her napkin. As she followed him back to the front hall, she calculated the odds on who her caller would be. Two to one it was Kane, she decided. He'd had all night to think, and he wasn't one to put off action unless he had something to gain by dawdling. Which, in this case, he didn't.

But the soft, slightly breathy voice on the other end of the line belonged to Paul Wintergreen. Alex shook her head ruefully. She had to be careful not to let herself get caught up in wishful thinking. It wasn't good legal practice.

Wintergreen Associates had offices in a renovated old building not far from downtown. Paul Wintergreen's office was a corner suite, sleek and contemporary except for an elaborately carved and gilded French Provincial desk set at a dramatic angle in the center of the room. He rose from behind it as his secretary showed her in. He was in his midthirties, she guessed, and not much taller than Alex's five seven. His hair was thinning, and even excellent tailoring could not entirely hide the softness around the waistline that in later years might become a paunch if he wasn't careful.

"Miss Jacobi, I'm very sorry about keeping you waiting yesterday." His voice was more intimate than it had sounded on the telephone, and his handshake was gentle, his palm lingering softly against her fingers.

Alex refrained from reminding him that he was paying for her time, whether he kept her busy or not.

"I'm glad you could come over this morning." He turned to the secretary. "Bring us coffee, please, Libby. And make a reservation for lunch at my club for Miss Jacobi and me. One o'clock, I think."

Alex took the chair he indicated beside the gracefully curved end of the desk. "Lunch would be very nice, Mr. Wintergreen, but it's certainly not necessary."

"On the contrary. It's the least I can do after keeping you waiting yesterday." He waved the secretary out of the room and went to sit behind his desk. "And it's Paul, please. If we're going to be working together..." He smiled. "I'm so glad Neville sent you, Alexandra. May I call you that?"

His smile was almost sweet. But there was a hint of cool calculation in his eyes that sent a chill down Alex's spine. What was it Kane had called Paul Wintergreen last night? Paul Playboy, that was it. She was beginning to see why.

Well, she reminded herself philosophically, she had found from long experience that the best way to handle clients with a tendency to be amorous was to get down to business, fast.

She took the file out of her briefcase and opened it on her lap. "I've reviewed your uncle's will, Mr. Wintergreen, and the paperwork that's already been done on the estate..."

He looked unhappy, but he didn't repeat the invitation to use his first name.

"...but I didn't see anything in the file about your cousin's threat to get the will overturned," Alex went on. "Do you have the papers relating to that? Did he write you a letter about his intention perhaps?"

Paul Wintergreen shook his head. "Oh, no. He hasn't been in touch with me about it, and I doubt he ever will be. You see, Ralph's a bit of a blowhard, that's all. He thinks he'll save face by making a fuss about the will, but when it all comes down to black and white he won't do anything."

Paul might well have been right, Alex thought. He certainly knew his cousin, which she did not. But on the other hand... "Why don't you tell me about him, anyway?" she said.

The picture of Ralph Wintergreen that emerged from Paul's description was not a flattering one. "Ne'er-do-well" was about the nicest thing Paul said about him. "Ralph's father was the black sheep of the family," he explained. "In fact, he was written out of Grandfather's will, so why Ralph thinks he has any claim at all on Uncle Geoffrey is beyond me. But he seems to think that Uncle Geoffrey promised him a full share. That's just what I've picked up from the talk I've heard around town, you understand."

"Promised him how?" Alex asked. "I mean, does Ralph say this promise was made on Geoffrey's death-bed, or at a party, or—"

"I wouldn't know. Over a chess game, I suppose. Ralph was always hanging about the house. But in any case, isn't it up to him to prove there was a promise? He can't just walk into court and say there was, can he?"

"It's doubtful he could make a case, unless he has witnesses."

Paul shook his head. "I can't think who they'd be. Uncle Geoffrey's butler is deaf as a post, and if anyone else was there whenever Ralph appeared, they promptly made an excuse and left. No one could stand him, partly because he was continually harping about money. I know Uncle Geoffrey was always writing to him about his financial troubles—"

Alarms went off inside Alex's head. "Ralph's money problems? But why would your uncle write to him if Ralph was always around the house?"

Paul shrugged. "Oh, Geoffrey was of the old school. He didn't believe that using the telephone was quite mannerly. If he wanted me to come to dinner with him, he'd send the chauffeur down to the office with a message."

Alex said slowly, "So there *are* letters to Ralph."

"Rafts of them, no doubt," Paul said disdainfully. "You have no idea how the old man would go on."

"And some of them are about money."

Paul nodded. "I'd say the subject came up regularly, knowing Ralph's habits."

Alex sighed. "And of course the letters are in Ralph's possession."

"I doubt he's still got them. Ralph's not the organized sort. He probably tossed them out before the ink was even dry, especially if he didn't like the advice."

Alex was not so sure. "Is there any way to find out for certain what was in those letters?"

"Copies, you mean? Of course. Geoffrey kept copies of everything." Paul was frowning. "What are you getting at, anyway? What's the problem? The will gave Ralph some cash. It's not as if he was left out altogether. So why is there any question about overturning it? He simply can't, can he?"

"It would seem on the surface he can't. But you see, if there *was* a promise made..."

Paul shook his head. "I can't imagine there was. Even if Uncle Geoffrey did say something of the sort, I'll bet he meant it to be sarcastic."

"Nevertheless, if there is the barest hint in even one of those letters of a promise to take care of Ralph's financial problems, or a suggestion that once Geoffrey was dead he'd have no more troubles, or even a reference to a discussion about Ralph's inheritance, anything like that, Ralph's lawyer can make the case that it was just like a codicil to the will."

"Like adding an additional paragraph after the will was finished?"

"Exactly."

"Good God," Paul said.

"And if it's there, I'd like to know it now, before this whole matter winds up in court." Alex closed the folder on her lap. "Where can I find Geoffrey's letters?"

"In our warehouse, stored with all the old business files. But you surely don't want to start on that until after lunch," Paul protested. "It's going to be quite a job."

She didn't realize how very correct Paul was until that afternoon, when she first saw the warehouse and the stack of cartons that contained Geoffrey Wintergreen's personal records. The pile filled nearly an entire bay of the warehouse's main floor.

Paul chewed his bottom lip and said, "Even I had no idea how many boxes there were. I had his files moved down here because I figured they'd be safer all together, where no one had easy access. But you can't work here, Alexandra."

Alex looked around the warehouse and was tempted to agree. Still, the place was relatively clean, and the lighting was bright enough. "There isn't any sense in hauling all this somewhere else."

He looked doubtful for a moment, but then his brow cleared. "Well, at least I can get you some help. I'll send a couple of secretaries...."

Alex shook her head. "I'm afraid they'd only be in the way, because I'll really have to look at each piece of paper myself. But if you could get me a long table and a decent office chair, and maybe someone with a strong back to move boxes, I'd appreciate it."

It was apparent to Alex as soon as she opened the first box that she was dealing with an orderly mind, one that had never allowed a single scrap of paper that might have some future value to be discarded. But the packing and moving of Geoffrey's files had created chaos in what must have once been a meticulously organized system. Every folder and every envelope was intact, she had no doubt of that. But it looked as if each packet of papers had been tossed into the boxes almost at random.

There were thousands of files covering the past forty years. Geoffrey had maintained an individual file for each company he dealt with, and within each category there were separate envelopes for orders he had placed, for paid bills, for cash receipts.

Also scattered at random among the boxes were folders full of letters. To Alex's dismay, however, they were organized by date, not by subject, so a letter to what appeared to be an old friend, congratulating him on another birthday, was right behind a complaint about the quality of food at Geoffrey's club, and directly ahead of a query about why the premium had gone up on his health-insurance policies....

Alex groaned. Considering the fastidious way Geoffrey had separated everything else, wouldn't it have been more reasonable to set up a separate folder for each one of his correspondents, rather than lump everything together by date?

Well, she'd probably end up going through every page, anyway, she reminded herself, not only to make sure a letter hadn't been misfiled, but to be certain all the estate's assets were perfectly appraised and accounted for. She'd just have to be more thorough than usual and read every single word. It wouldn't be the first time she'd tackled a needle-in-the-haystack search.

It was hours later—she wasn't certain how many, for she'd started counting time only in terms of boxes completed—when she heard the warehouse door creak open. No doubt it was Paul, she thought, coming back to check on her progress or to renew the dinner invitation she'd politely turned down earlier. She might just change her mind, though, she decided. He had been a pleasant companion over lunch, and he hadn't exactly chased her around his desk this morning. Besides, she had some questions for him.

She gingerly stretched her neck muscles, stiffened by hours of sitting over a pile of papers, and peered over the wall of boxes.

But it wasn't Paul, it was Kane, almost silent-footed in rubber-soled shoes, who was crossing the warehouse toward the pool of light where she sat. He stopped directly in front of her, stuck his fingers into the pockets of his jeans and surveyed the mess. His voice was careless. "Hi. Having fun?"

"Loads," Alex said crisply. "What are you doing here?"

"Oh, I checked at the Guest House, and they said you'd gone missing hours ago. So I called up Paul to ask where he'd hidden your body, and he told me you were here." He looked around. "I must give him credit. This is much more original than strangling you and covering your corpse with leaves. You'll die of boredom, and no one will ever think of looking here."

"Very funny." She turned back to her stack of letters. "Why would he want to strangle me, anyway? He likes me."

"I'm not surprised. Paul is instantly disposed to like anything wearing a skirt. Of course, if he saw you at the moment, he might not be so impressed. You look like a coal miner."

Alex glared through her lashes at him without even raising her head. "Uncle Geoffrey didn't believe in modern conveniences like photocopy machines. Ordinary old carbon paper was good enough for him." She looked distastefully at her grimy hands. Even her manicured nails were rimmed with black.

Kane picked up a page from the stack she had already inspected. "Of course, a good proportion of this stuff predates Xerox," he observed.

"Did you come down to help?"

He set the paper down as if it had burned him. "Of course not. But I figured you might want company for dinner."

And you, Alex thought, *are ready to deal.*

Well, that was fair enough. But though she certainly wouldn't turn down the opportunity to talk to him, nothing said she had to look eager for his company. "On my expense account again, I suppose?"

"Oh, no," Kane said airily. "My treat."

That genuinely startled her. Her fountain pen slipped out of her fingers and left a blob of ink on the legal pad at her elbow.

"You don't need to look astounded," he complained. "I do have gentlemanly instincts once in a while."

Alex didn't want to get into that discussion. She just said calmly, "I am a little hungry, now that you mention it." She gathered up her notes and her briefcase and pondered the wisdom of leaving the papers on the table or packing them all back up again. Then she remembered what Paul had said about no one having easy access to the warehouse. Besides, anyone who'd wanted to could have opened the boxes at any time, she told herself.

Kane held the warehouse door for her. "You don't mind, do you?" he asked earnestly. "My opening doors, I mean. Once in a while a hard-line feminist does object, I know."

"I'll consider it merely courtesy. Where are we going?"

"My place."

She paused with the key Paul had given her still in the lock of the warehouse door.

"Don't panic. It's just that since I'm unemployed at the moment..."

"And not on expense account any longer," Alex inserted.

"...I'm entertaining with pasta and cheap white wine these days. Hope you don't mind."

It was silly to question his motives, she told herself. This was a negotiation, not a date. What difference did it make where they sat down to talk or what they ate? "It depends on whether you know how to cook pasta. Do you?"

"I'm getting better at it."

Alex shrugged. "Then I'm willing to give it a try." He opened the passenger door of the Ferrari, but she shook her head. "I'll follow you."

Rush hour was apparently past, for traffic was light. She was astonished to see that the road she had traveled yesterday in the fog was not the ordinary highway she'd thought. In places it ran within yards of the edge of Lake Superior. She paled at the memory of the way she had taken those curves without any idea of what lay just beyond the edge of the road.

But it was beautiful, she had to admit. The waves were catching and shattering the last soft rays of light as the sun set behind her, and the water shimmered with vibrant shades of orchid and rose and violet. More than once Alex would have liked to pull off to the side of the road and just watch the lake and the sunset for a while, or pick a few of the gloriously abundant wildflowers at the roadside. But ahead of her the Ferrari was twisting around curves at a ridiculous speed, so she put her foot down a little harder and stopped watching the landscape. After all, she still had work to do. Pence Whitfield had not sent her to Duluth to admire the scenery.

She was half a minute behind him. By the time she pulled her car into the driveway at Inglenook, Kane was leaning into the back of the Ferrari to gather up grocery bags. Alex went to help, but before she could make the offer she saw something that drove all other concerns out of her mind.

In the driver's-side window of the Ferrari was a For Sale sign. She stared at it for half a minute in blank astonishment. "Why are you selling your car?"

Kane retrieved a head of lettuce that had escaped from the bag and handed it to her. "It's pretty impractical. Terrible gas mileage, only two passengers . . ."

"I thought that was the whole point of having a sports car."

"And no room to haul driftwood, either."

"Now I understand the problem." Alex's voice was dry.

Kane shifted the bag of groceries and grinned at her.

Don't be silly, Alex told herself. *You've seen him smile before.*

But not like this, as if he had focused all the energy within him into one warm stream and was beaming it directly at her. The smile lit his eyes with a wicked sparkle and drew interesting lines all over his face.

"Maybe I'll get a dune buggy, instead."

"Gee, that'll be comfortable in the winter."

Kane shrugged. "When it gets cold I'll stay home by my fire." He waved casually at the house next door; from the corner of her eye Alex saw a crisp white curtain drop back into place. Eleanor was on duty again, she thought.

The side door where Alex had left her card just the day before was less than thirty feet from the lake. Twenty feet out and ten straight down, she corrected, studying the way the lawn sloped down to the concrete seawall. She'd had no idea she was so close to the water; yesterday's fog had been too thick to tell.

She stood there holding the lettuce and staring at the lake. The glorious pastels had given way to pale blue and gray as the light softened even more, and bobbing in the water, a hundred or so feet out from shore, was the funniest-looking duck Alex had ever seen.

Kane had followed her gaze. "It's a loon," he said. "He'll probably go under any minute now, fishing for his dinner." He pushed the door open and stepped back to let her precede him.

Alex was reluctant to leave the view behind. But the moment she stepped into the house she realized it had been a foolish thought. The lakeside wall of the kitchen had a big uncurtained window that framed the identical view, and beside it was a small table and a couple of chairs. On the table was a yellow legal pad, the top sheet covered with writing; Kane scooped it up, dumped it into a drawer and set the bag of groceries in its place.

"If you'd like to wash your hands, there's a powder room around the corner," he said, pointing.

Alex almost told him that what she'd really like to do was read what was on the legal pad. She was certain it would have simplified her job. But she meekly went off to scrub the carbon from her hands, instead.

The tiny powder room was tucked under the bend of the staircase. Alex was startled at first to see the wicker basket of frilly guest towels on the vanity, and the crystal dish full of tiny carved hand soaps. Kane didn't seem the sort to bother with such details. Then she remembered the woman's voice she'd heard during that telephone call. Of course he had female guests, Alex told herself. But she couldn't help but wonder a little who had arranged the delicate details.

A pot of water was steaming on the range when she returned to the kitchen with every hair back in place and her hands restored to their customary color. Kane handed her a long-stemmed glass of white wine.

Alex sipped it with appreciation. It might not be an expensive vintage, but it was good. "Can I help?"

"You can make the salads."

"Great." She set the wineglass down beside the sink and began to unwrap the head of lettuce. "I'm too hungry to stand on ceremony."

"That's the lake effect. All the fresh air around here builds appetites."

"I'd have thought it was the warehouse effect myself. Shoving all those boxes around would give anyone an appetite. But it is a beautiful lake . . ."

"It's got you already," Kane said with satisfaction.

" . . . as lakes go," Alex finished. "I see why the road is marked as a scenic highway. It wasn't very scenic yesterday, what with the fog."

"It's too bad your first sight of the water was blocked. It's really a beautiful view as you come into town."

"I wasn't worried about views—I was just trying to keep from getting lost."

"In Duluth? How can you get lost?"

Alex shrugged. "I managed."

Kane salted the water and started to dump fresh fettuccine into the kettle. Before she could stop herself, Alex had grabbed the package out of his hand. "Not like that," she said. "Add it slowly so the water doesn't stop boiling, or it'll be soggy."

He looked surprised. "And where did the consummate attorney learn to cook?"

"Everybody has to eat." She stirred the pasta and handed him the spoon. "Besides, I grew up in a restaurant."

He frowned a little.

Now why had she told him that? Alex wondered. She didn't try to keep Gus and his restaurant a secret, but she also didn't go out of her way to volunteer the information. There were people who considered her old neighborhood to be the wrong side of the tracks, and some had held it against her.

"Of course," he said. "I've been to Jacobi's a time or two."

"You amaze me." She finished tearing lettuce and began arranging it on a pair of china plates.

"And here I am cooking for you—and using the recipe off the back of the fettuccine box." Kane looked a little worried. "Maybe I should throw in the spoon while I still can."

Alex shook her head. "I didn't say I was any kind of chef. Actually I never had much hands-on training at all, but I watched everything. My father always said he had no intention of letting me end up in the restaurant business." And that was enough of her history, too, she thought. "I like your house. It's cute. Did you rent it furnished or something?"

"No, it's mine. My great-aunt Tess left it to me, pots and pans and all."

"Oh, that explains why you chose Duluth. I couldn't figure out what brought you here. I know you said it was the lake, but still . . ." She picked up a tomato. "Do you have a really sharp knife?"

Kane reached around her and into a drawer. For a moment his arm was almost circling her. He sniffed and said, "What's that scent you're wearing?"

Alex raised her eyebrows. "It's either the floral soap from your powder room or the dust from the warehouse. Why do you ask?"

Kane laughed. "It's not dust, so don't worry. Are you having any trouble keeping Paul Playboy under control?"

Alex was suddenly and perversely unwilling to admit that she'd paid any attention to his warning. "I don't know why you call him that. He invited me to lunch, that's all." She shrugged. "He seems to be a sweet guy."

"Right. He's been married three times, too."

She chopped a cucumber into cubes and said coolly, "I am a grown woman, Kane. Don't you think I know how to look after myself as well as any of your male colleagues?"

He drew back as if the question had been a hot object tossed straight at his face. "Of course," he said. He reached into the refrigerator for a container of cream, and his voice was a bit muffled. "But then I find it difficult to treat you exactly as I would any male colleague."

She should have at least appreciated his honesty, but in fact the admission annoyed her. "Why?" She knew she sounded touchy, and that made her even more irritated. "I'm as hardworking and professional as any man, and—"

Kane interrupted. "I think it's because I've never had the urge to kiss any one of my male colleagues, Alex. Now you, on the other hand..."

Her mouth dropped open. She couldn't help it.

Kane gave her a lazy smile and added, "Hand me the fettuccine box, would you? I need to check my recipe."

CHAPTER FOUR

IT TOOK ALEX half a minute to get her breath back, and then she managed to laugh. "That's all very amusing," she said. "But if you don't mind . . ."

Kane looked over his shoulder at her. He had just raised a forkful of fettuccine to test whether it was done; the pasta hung suspended in midair, dripping. "What's so amusing about it? I wasn't joking."

"Oh, for heaven's sake," Alex said impatiently, "I know it wasn't a joke. It was a negotiating trick, and I wish you'd cut it out. That sort of comment just isn't appropriate between colleagues, Kane."

He nodded. "I agree. That's only one of the reasons I'm having so much fun now that I'm not associated with Pence Whitfield anymore. Here, do you think this pasta is done?"

Reluctantly she moved closer to him. The kitchen wasn't large to start with, but it seemed to Alex that it had shrunk remarkably in the past few minutes.

She bit down on the fragment of fettuccine he held out and nodded her approval. Then, though she wanted immediately to scuttle back across the room, she forced herself to stay put and watch as he drained the pasta and stirred in cream and parmesan cheese.

It was silly, she told herself, to let a casual comment throw her so off-balance. And it was more than just silly—it was insane to let herself react like this to him. It wasn't as if he'd suddenly started exuding hormones, after all; he'd always been an attractive man. There was no reason the mention of a kiss should make her any more aware of that fact.

"Would you hold the plates?" Kane asked. He dished up the fettuccine and Alex carried the plates over to the small table. She fussed with the salads, the napkins and the silverware while Kane waited patiently to hold her chair. She thought she saw a gleam of humorous appreciation in his eyes as he finally seated himself across from her.

So much for his statement that it hadn't been a joke, Alex thought. Of course it was just a game to him. He was toying with her, seeing what kind of reaction he could provoke. It certainly didn't mean he had any intention whatever of actually trying to kiss her.

Still, the idea that he was amused by her uneasiness annoyed her beyond all reason, and her voice was crisp as she shook out her napkin and picked up her fork. "What do you want from Pence Whitfield, Kane?"

His dark eyebrows lifted a fraction. "To make me come back, you mean?"

At least he was taking her question seriously this time, Alex thought. He wasn't pretending not to understand what she was talking about.

Kane refilled her wineglass from the bottle at his elbow. "I don't quite know. What are they offering?"

Alex wasn't fooled by the careless tone of his voice. "That's not the way it works. It's like poker, and with this hand it's your turn to open."

He smiled and began patiently twisting fettuccine strands around his fork. "Then tell them I'm still looking at my cards, and when I decide I'll let you know."

It was more than she'd expected; at least now he'd admitted an interest in negotiating.

"And it's not as if I don't have time to consider it," Kane went on. "From the looks of that warehouse, you'll be here for months."

The reminder of the sheer volume of Geoffrey Wintergreen's files made Alex want to groan. "Maybe. And I might find what I'm looking for tomorrow."

He smiled a little. "And go rushing straight back to Minneapolis before I've had a chance to think things over? I doubt it."

He was entirely too sure of himself, Alex decided. Perhaps it was time to give him a warning. "Just don't wait too long. The longer you're up here, out of touch, the more chance that Pence Whitfield will learn to do without you."

He looked thoughtful. "Or find someone to take my place."

"Someone could, you know. Doesn't the idea bother you? Surely you're not conceited enough to think you're indispensable, Kane." There was a delicious note of irony in telling him that, she thought, especially since Neville Morgan had practically admitted he was irreplaceable.

"Oh, no," Kane said easily. "I'm very aware that I'm a hack attorney. There's one like me on every street corner."

"I didn't say that, either, and you know it. You're good, and you've been lucky, but..."

Kane's eyebrows arched.

Alex went on stubbornly, "I mean you're lucky to be associated with Pence Whitfield. There are plenty of people who would love to be in your shoes, Kane, and some of them are well qualified."

"And some of them wouldn't hesitate to stab me in the back if it would get them there," he said.

"That's true, too. The longer you sit up here contemplating your future—"

"The less likely I am to have one? That's an intriguing thought. How about you, Alex? You're out of contact at the moment, too. Don't you worry about somebody stabbing you in the back while you're gone?" He thought over what he'd said and frowned. "That didn't track quite right, but I'm sure you know what I mean."

Gus had said almost the same thing, Alex reflected. Something about being careful to stay visible so the senior partners wouldn't forget how valuable she was.

She smiled at Kane. "I'm not worried. If I manage to bring you back into the fold, my position will be unassailable."

"And all because of me," Kane murmured. "You know, Alex, you certainly have a way of making a man feel you can't do without him."

Alex choked on her wine.

There was a telltale twitch at the corner of Kane's mouth. "And of course that Pence Whitfield can't, either," he added smoothly. "Are you certain they don't have an opening offer for me to consider?"

Alex set her glass down and picked up her fork again. She looked at her plate and drew lines in the cooling cheese sauce for a minute, then raised her eyes to his. "As a matter of fact, they do."

Kane leaned forward in his chair, obviously interested. "Now we're getting somewhere."

"Mr. Morgan said if you're doing penance for messing up the Quadrangle affair, he'd forgive you. That's the extent of the deal."

Kane laughed and got up to fill the coffeepot.

"So are you doing penance?" she asked.

"Of course not." He started the pot brewing and came back to his chair.

Alex propped her elbows on the edge of the table and prompted, "What happened to the Quadrangle deal, anyway?"

"I'm sure you've already heard the details."

"Well, it has gotten a lot of discussion around the office." Her voice was casual. Kane didn't need to know that it was her secretary who'd filled her in on the office scuttlebutt, after Neville Morgan had given her this assignment. "And nobody understands what you were thinking. It was a really big deal, Kane. After months of maneuvering, Quadrangle was in position to take over its biggest competitor. And yet at the last minute, Quadrangle's chairman calls a press conference and announces that on advice of counsel—that's you—he's calling off the whole deal."

Kane nodded. "Sounds about right." He picked up the plates and took them to the sink, then returned with two empty coffee mugs and a plate of chocolate cookies. "Have one," he urged. "Eleanor made them."

Alex refused to be distracted. "There are two camps when it comes to interpretations. The first group thinks that something turned out to have been wrong with the deal all along—in which case you have a vague look of incompetence, because you failed to see it earlier."

"Ouch," Kane said. "I hadn't heard that one."

"Who would dare tell you? The second group thinks the deal was so big you simply lost your nerve."

The coffeepot sighed and Kane got up to fill their cups. "How about theory three—that I was bribed?"

"I haven't heard anybody saying that."

"That's a relief."

"Were you?"

"Compared to the fees for putting the deal together, who'd have had enough money to bribe me to cancel it?"

"But of course the fees went to the firm," Alex said thoughtfully. "The bribe would be strictly private."

"Hmm. I'll have to remember that if the opportunity ever comes up. Cream and sugar?"

Alex shook her head. "So what really happened, Kane?"

"Oh, it was cold feet," he said airily. "Let's take our coffee into the living room where we can be comfortable."

She had caught a glimpse of the room earlier; it ran the full width of the house, and where the walls weren't lined with bookshelves they were knotty pine—casual and warm-looking. The room had obviously been designed for privacy; there was only one small window facing the street, but the opposite wall, the one that looked out over the lake, was entirely glass. No neighboring houses were in view, which made the cottage seem all alone on the north shore. And now that the sun had set, the water looked cold and gray and forbidding once more.

She chose an overstuffed swivel rocker and turned its back to the window, watching as Kane knelt on the hearth to start the fire. Flames licked at the kindling and in mere moments grew into a bright little blaze. The room had seemed perfectly comfortable when she came in; still, the first waves of heat were welcome, and she was touched that he'd remembered her wish for a fire the previous night.

She stretched her toes out toward the flames. "I don't believe you. That you got scared, I mean."

Kane sounded genuinely surprised. "Oh, it wasn't *my* cold feet that caused the problem—it was Quadrangle's. The chairman took one last look at what the deal was going to do to his balance sheet, and the debt load scared him out of his wits."

Alex sipped her coffee thoughtfully. "You expect me to believe you couldn't persuade him it would all work out?"

For a long moment, Kane simply looked at her, and Alex thought she saw respect spring to life in his eyes. He shook his head cheerfully. "I could hardly convince him, since I'm the one who told him to take one last look at the debt load."

It was far from what she'd expected to hear. Alex stared into the fire, considering. Finally she said very carefully, "You deliberately sabotaged your own deal?"

"He ended up with a better one, Alex. The opposition scrambled so hard to stop the takeover that they're in a phenomenal mess, and Quadrangle can sit back and pick their business off in pieces at the chairman's leisure, without worrying about the debt he'd have taken on to acquire the whole firm."

"And you let everybody think you chickened out."

"That's right, because the longer the opposition keeps thinking that, the less they'll be on guard. Of course, the accountants and the business types who came up with the takeover idea in the first place are a bit unhappy, but..." He shrugged.

"That's diabolical."

"It's looking out for my client, Alex. In this case, the best deal ended up being no deal at all."

Neville Morgan was right, Alex thought. Kane was plotting something or, more likely, simply waiting for the truth to come out so that the firm would receive him as a hero. Perhaps he was already a little tired of the isolation of Duluth, and that was why he'd told her about the Quadrangle affair, knowing the story would swiftly get back to the senior partners.

Alex frowned a little, suddenly uncomfortable with the idea. It looked as if she was going to wind up being a pipeline, after all.

Kane went outside for another log. Alex walked over to the window to look at the almost-black water, and shivered a little in the gust of cool air he'd let in. In the winter, she thought, with the waves pounding and the wind howling off the lake and snow swirling everywhere, this would not be a hospitable place.

"Are you still cold?" Kane asked when he returned. "Move closer to the fire."

Alex left her position by the window and did as he suggested. "I was just thinking about winter." She shot a look at him and decided to try out her theory that he was already feeling isolated. "Won't it be dreadful out here? How are you going to bear it?"

"The house has stood up to the weather for forty years. I don't imagine it'll go on strike this winter."

"With the ice and snow, how will you get around? Trade the Ferrari in for a snowmobile?"

"That's a thought. But snow removal is really quite efficient up here. At least that's what Aunt Tess used to say."

Alex brushed her fingertips across the afghan draped over the back of the couch, and conjured up a mental image of the lady who'd made it. Each square was tiny and intricate and made up of a rainbow of odd colors of yarn—bits left over from other projects, she imagined. "Aunt Tess probably didn't go outside between October and May."

Kane grinned. "Obviously you didn't know Aunt Tess."

Alex sat down on the couch. "So tell me about her." It wasn't that she particularly wanted to know about Aunt Tess, but she suspected she might find out something more about Kane.

He moved Alex's coffee cup to a more convenient table and sat down at the opposite end of the couch, his back against the high arm. His cup was cradled in one hand, and the other trailed across the soft wool afghan as if simply touching it brought back memories. "She was my grandfather's sister, but she was so much younger she was actually of my father's generation. She never married, and she always lived alone, except when she brought me up here every summer. She always said it was her duty to my father to take over one-third of his burden of kids now and then."

"It doesn't sound as if she enjoyed the experience."

Kane smiled. "Tess always did her best to sound hard-boiled about it, true. She wouldn't take either of my sisters, because she insisted boys were less trouble."

Alex's eyebrows went up a fraction.

"She said boys didn't need entertaining, and they didn't care if they had baths and regular meals. And she was right—I didn't need any of that stuff. I had a wonderful time just walking on that rocky beach. Of course, the main reason I enjoyed it was that Tess taught me all about fossils and shells and tides and—"

"Driftwood, I suppose?"

His eyes gleamed. "That, too. We found a gorgeous piece of weathered walnut once. Tess swore it was part of the *Edmund Fitzgerald* wreckage, but I suppose it was probably just a piece of some classy cabin cruiser. More coffee?"

Alex shook her head.

"We'd raid the garden when we were hungry—which I seem to recall was most of the time. The lake effect, you know."

"I seem to have heard about that somewhere," Alex murmured.

"Have you ever eaten a tomato still warm from the sun? You just pick it and bite into it like a plum, and juice runs everywhere."

"I haven't had the pleasure."

"You don't know what you're missing. At the end of the summer I'd be wiry and brown and six inches taller, and Tess would put me on the bus and tell me that at least I'd been less of a nuisance than usual, and then she'd wave goodbye and blink a lot...."

"In other words," Alex said lazily, "the woman was a fraud. So what did she do the rest of the year when she didn't have you around to adore?"

"She was a librarian. And she almost single-handedly set up and ran the local hospice for the terminally ill, and she was very active in her church. So if you think she didn't set a pampered toe outside her door in the winter, Alex, I've got news for you."

"I concede that Tess's high opinion of the snow removal is probably valid. Still, I can't imagine it being all that pleasant when there's a snowstorm howling off the lake."

"And ice floes building up offshore," Kane added calmly. "Did you know this is the only place outside of the Arctic Circle that honestly has blue ice?"

Alex shuddered. "If you've only been here in the summers, how do you know you can handle it?"

"Would Tess steer me wrong?" He stretched his feet out toward the fire.

"With all those visits up here," Alex said slowly, "I'll bet you really do know the Wintergreens. More than just by name and reputation, I mean."

He nodded. "Paul's a couple of years older than I am."

Just a couple? Alex thought. That surprised her; she'd have said, from appearances, that the difference was more like half a dozen years.

"And Ralph lived in a rough sort of neighborhood, so we were never best buddies. But yes, I know them. How do you feel about your case now? Do you think Geoffrey Wintergreen promised Ralph a full share?"

"I don't have an opinion. I've hardly scratched the surface of the papers."

Kane got up to get the coffeepot. "I didn't ask about the papers. I wanted to know what your gut feeling is."

"How would I know?"

He paused with the pot suspended above his cup. "You don't have feelings? Dammit, Alex, you spent the afternoon with all that's left of Geoffrey. You should have some sense of his personality by now."

"I certainly can't make predictions based on a few cartons of personal papers."

He tipped his head to one side and studied her. "You've been hanging around with Neville Morgan so long I'll bet if you cut yourself you wouldn't even bleed— you'd spew out whereases and heretofores instead. Did you have to take law school so awfully seriously?"

"I didn't think it was a lark," Alex said stiffly. "You obviously have an opinion on the Wintergreen case. Could I possibly prevail on you to share it with me?"

Kane stirred restlessly and settled back against the deep cushions. "I think Geoffrey did. Leave reasonable doubt, I mean."

"Well, that's interesting. But unless you can come up with something concrete, I hope you'll pardon me if I don't act on your intuition."

He gave her a cheerful grin. "Then you don't want my help, after all?"

There seemed no safe answer to that, so Alex glanced at her wristwatch. "My goodness, is that the time? I'd better be getting back to the Guest House before they lock the doors."

"I wouldn't want you to miss your sleep." He walked her out to her car.

The air had turned misty again, though it was not the dense fog of the day before, only a ghostly drift of haze here and there. The night was chilly, and Alex shivered a little, despite her linen jacket.

Kane carefully closed the door, then tapped on the window. Alex rolled it down, and he leaned against the car, arms folded. "Call me when you get back to the Guest House, will you?" he asked. "Just so I know you made it back safely."

Alex bristled a little. She stared straight ahead, her hands already on the steering wheel. "I'm perfectly capable of getting myself there in one piece, Kane."

"That's good." His voice was gentle. "By the way, before you self-destruct with irritation at my sexist attitudes, if you were a man I probably would have asked the same thing. The mist can be tricky on the low spots in the highway."

She swallowed hard and admitted to herself that it was rather nice of him to be concerned.

"But I wouldn't have done this, of course." His fingertips brushed her chin, gently turning her face toward him. Alex's eyes widened in alarm, but before she could pull back, Kane had leaned into the car and pressed his mouth to hers.

His lips lingered on hers. Then he pulled back, smiled at her and said softly, "Drive carefully. And call me."

THE GUEST HOUSE was still and almost completely dark. The front door was locked, and Alex suffered a moment of pure panic before she realized that the pool of light she could see through the stained-glass panels wasn't merely a security measure. A form moved across the hall, blocking the light for a moment before the lock clicked and the night desk clerk, paperback book in hand, let her in.

The whole house was silent. Her room was pleasantly warm, and the coverlet was already turned down and the pillows fluffed. Alex undressed and dropped her carbon-smudged suit into a bag to be sent out for cleaning, then sat down on the edge of the bed to brush her hair. She eyed the telephone. It would be rude not to call Kane after he'd asked. It wasn't as though he didn't have a good reason for the request; the mist *had* been unpredictable and the highway markings hard to see. Besides, not to call would put too much importance on that silly kiss, wouldn't it? He might think she was sulking because of it, or playing hard-to-get.

She checked her address book and dialed his number. But the instant he answered and she heard that husky sensual voice, she regretted the act. All she was accomplishing by calling him was to pander to his ego, and the man certainly didn't need any more of that!

But it was too late to hang up. "Reporting in as requested," she said crisply.

"How was the mist?"

"Tricky."

"Next time I'll just suggest you stay."

"It wasn't that tricky."

He started to laugh, and Alex could almost see the way his eyes crinkled at the corners.

"Relax, Alexandra. The lake doesn't deliver fog on demand, you know. Sleep well."

Alex drew a breath in order to retort, but he had already hung up. And no doubt drifted straight off into a dreamless peaceful sleep, too, she told herself furiously half an hour later as she tossed and turned and punched at her pillow.

That kiss had been just another from his bag of tricks, she thought. It was an old technique, too, nothing original about it. He simply told his victim exactly what he was going to do, then waited patiently till she was off guard and the threat forgotten before carrying it out. It had twice the effect that way.

"At least it had in this case," Alex muttered, "since I'm still very much awake."

But it was nothing short of stupid to take it so seriously, she warned herself. So what if the man could kiss like an angel? Whatever Kane's goal was, it certainly wasn't seduction. If he was the sort to go after any available female, every secretary in the firm would have known it, and Sharon would have warned her.

Not that Alex would have needed the warning; if Kane had that kind of appetite, she'd have suspected it herself long ago. That kind of attitude didn't stay hidden long when people worked together. But in her experience, he'd always been all business, with never a hint of suggestiveness—at least not until she'd come to Duluth. Even at that Christmas party, when there had been a fair number of Pence Whitfield employees making fools of themselves in dim corners, Kane had been quite content to talk business....

It had been the first Christmas she had worked for Pence Whitfield. Alex had finished her work with Kane's team and rotated on to another of the specialties as part of her orientation, and she hadn't seen him again until the party.

The Christmas party was the firm's biggest event of the year. The largest ballroom of one of the elegant downtown hotels was rented and no expense spared on catering or entertainment. That year there'd been a very popular band, and so nearly every one of the staff was present, from senior partners to paralegals to receptionists, most with spouses or dates, enjoying the rare break from work.

Alex came late, alone, and straight from the office, where she'd changed her clothes. She was just picking up her glass of tonic water from the bar when Kane joined her, ordered another drink and asked if she was enjoying the party.

"I just got here, so I haven't had a chance to decide," Alex said. "I didn't know it would be so big or so noisy."

"Oh, you've missed the best part. It's all strictly downhill from here. Someone will pinch one of the senior partners' wives and get his face slapped, and someone else will fall headfirst into the punch bowl. We let our hair down so seldom that it's not a pretty sight when we do."

"Just as well I'm not planning to stay, then," Alex said.

Kane's gaze skimmed over her emerald-green cocktail dress. "Another date?"

"No. Just a deskful of work."

"That seems a shame."

"Why? If the party is a waste of time, why not accomplish something worthwhile, instead?" Alex sipped her tonic water.

Kane took his drink from the bartender and leaned against the bar while he stirred it.

He didn't seem to be in any hurry to go back to whichever group he had been part of, Alex thought. She took a deep breath and ventured, "Anyway, if you've got a minute... I'd been hoping to run into you."

His eyebrows arched slightly. "Were you?"

"Yes. I wanted to ask how the Reynolds case turned out. I know you pulled it off, of course, but I want the details."

For a moment she thought the noise had overwhelmed her voice, for he didn't answer. Then he put down his cocktail stick and said, "Shall we find somewhere quieter to discuss it?"

He steered her to a little nook at the edge of the ballroom where the sound of the band was less overwhelming, and for the next twenty minutes she quizzed him about the case. Long before her last scrap of curiosity was satisfied, Alex was beginning to suspect that his patience was wearing thin, so she thanked him, apologized for bringing business into a party and excused herself to go back to work.

Kane had said, "Think nothing of it. It's the most fun I've had all evening." Alex didn't entirely believe him; in fact, as she was leaving the party a few minutes later she saw him dancing with Neville Morgan's daughter, Lisle, and he seemed to be enjoying himself. Still, if he'd been the sort to take advantage of any woman who happened to be handy, he'd had a perfect opportunity that night— an isolated little nook in a dimly lit room, in the middle of a party where no one was paying attention.

And tonight, with all kinds of chances, he'd waited till she was in her car before he'd even touched her. That was certainly not the action of a man with seduction in mind.

She had nothing to be concerned about.

CHAPTER FIVE

ALEX SPENT FRIDAY in the warehouse. She got through nine cartons of Geoffrey's papers, added seventeen questions for Paul to the list she'd started earlier and didn't catch a glimpse of Kane.

At noon she'd taken the picnic lunch that Mrs. Keith had packed for her down to a small waterfront park near the warehouse and dutifully admired the view of the aerial lift bridge, which was Duluth's most prominent landmark, while she munched on cheese and fruit and crusty French bread. She'd ignored most of what was in the small wicker basket—there was enough food for two. She wondered if Mrs. Keith, too, had half expected Kane to turn up at mealtime.

When Alex returned to the Guest House in the early evening, she tried to call him. When there wasn't any answer, she had dinner in her room and worked on a progress report on the Wintergreen case. She planned to fax it to Neville Morgan first thing Monday morning.

There was no sense in even starting a similar memo on the Kane Forrestal business, she told herself as she got ready for bed, since there was no progress to report.

But Saturday morning, when she was at the warehouse and halfway through her third carton of the day, a noise like a hammer hitting the warehouse door drew her attention away from Geoffrey's account of his dispute with a roofing contractor and back to the present.

Her first thought was that if someone was trying to break in to the warehouse, he was bound to succeed; the lock couldn't possibly stand up to much of an assault. And once he was in... well, no burglar expected to find a defenseless female in a warehouse in the middle of a Saturday morning; he probably expected the whole district to be empty if the noise he was making was any indication.

"Dammit, Alex, are you in there?" It was almost a bellow, and she leapt to her feet and rushed to the door.

Kane was on the threshold just raising his fist again when she twisted the key in the double dead-bolt lock and pulled the door open. "Yes," she said.

He was wearing khaki shorts and sneakers and a dark blue polo shirt, and his hair looked as if it hadn't been combed. "Can't you at least answer your door?" he said, sounding disgruntled. "Last time it wasn't even locked."

"And you walked right in. If you think about it, you might realize why it was locked this time."

"You don't want me?"

"Of course I—" She stopped the instant she saw the sparkle in his eyes. "It's not personal, Kane. All that talk about finding my corpse made me realize that not everyone wandering around the warehouse district is apt to be an upstanding citizen like you."

"Thank you, I'm so flattered my heart is racing—or maybe that's still the effect of seeing your car outside and wondering why you weren't anywhere around."

"Well, I'm glad to hear you'd be worried if I went missing."

"I'd be a lot more than worried. I'd be a prime suspect." He wandered across to the pool of light in her makeshift office and sat down on the end of the long table, swinging his feet. "It's Saturday," he pointed out.

"I know."

"And you're steadily chomping your way through these boxes. Didn't anybody ever teach you to play?"

"I'm not paid to play. The sooner I finish this job—"

"The sooner you can concentrate on me?"

He wasn't far off, but Alex didn't feel like admitting that.

Kane went on. "I assumed you'd go back to Minneapolis for the weekend."

"Did you now?"

"That's why I got so worried when your secretary called me."

"Sharon called you? What—"

"She tried to catch you at the Guest House, but all the phone lines seemed to be busy."

"That's no way to run a hotel," Alex said.

"She even thought about faxing the news to you—do you really have a fax machine installed in your room?"

"Why shouldn't I?"

"Oh, I expected you to think of it. I just didn't believe any hotel around here had given in to the craze. I may have to move farther north yet to escape the technological revolution."

Alex's tone was verging on dangerous. "Do you have a message for me or not, Kane?"

"Oh, yes. Sharon couldn't actually use the fax because she was at home, not in the office. But she wanted you to know... Let me get this straight." He pulled a slip of paper from the hip pocket of his shorts and carefully unfolded it. "Joanna had a boy."

Alex closed her eyes in relief. That was good; Joanna had wanted a boy. Of course, Alex had been thinking more in terms of Neville Morgan having a fit because she hadn't phoned the office yesterday, or of someone on the team playing politics with her job behind her back....

Damn Kane and his insinuations, anyway, she thought. Nobody was going to be trampling on her territory just because she was out of the office for a few days! She should have expected the message to be about the baby. She hoped Joanna was fine, and the baby healthy.

Kane watched her with interest. "Trying to remember who Joanna is?"

"I know perfectly well who she is."

"Your sister?"

"I haven't got one. Why do you want to know, anyway?"

Kane snapped his fingers. "I've got it—she's a surrogate mother. You'd like a baby, but you've decided you haven't time to actually produce one yourself, so—"

"She's a very good friend," Alex snapped. "Did Sharon tell you if the baby's healthy?"

"Let's see. He's just fine, she said, and...wait. Did she say six pounds or six feet? If he's got six—"

"I'll call her myself."

He laughed and handed over the note. In small painstakingly precise script, he had recorded the baby's vital statistics and name.

"Brandon James Adler," Alex murmured. "That's certainly a mouthful."

"I hope the poor kid doesn't stutter. Don't worry about my services. I'll send you a bill for the secretarial time."

Alex sat down again and picked up Geoffrey's letter to the roofing contractor. "Are you certain you wouldn't settle for lunch? I could stand a break."

"A break?" Kane's foot stopped swinging. "You mean you're planning to spend the afternoon here, too?"

"Don't give me a holier-than-thou lecture, Kane. You've worked a few Saturday afternoons, I'm sure."

"In my previous life, yes," he agreed cheerfully. "But even then I never would have missed an opportunity like this one. Just think, Alex. You can spend the afternoon with me, and even Neville Morgan would agree that you're working."

The really funny thing was that he was right, Alex thought, and it didn't matter what Kane wanted to do; Neville would still smile approvingly. "You win," she said, and tossed down Geoffrey's letter.

"Come on," Kane ordered. He eyed her moss-green suit and said hopefully, "Do you have decent clothes hidden somewhere? Jeans? Walking shoes?"

"Some. Why? What do you have in mind?"

"I'm going to teach you the fine art of beachcombing."

Alex smothered a groan. She ought to have anticipated that.

She followed him back to the Guest House. She missed a couple of traffic lights that the Ferrari surged through, and by the time she pulled into the parking lot, Kane was leaning against the door of his car, ankles crossed and arms folded on his chest. "I thought you got lost again," he accused.

"I considered it."

"But then I realized that someone as devoted to duty as you, Alex, would never run out on a case, no matter how challenging it turned out to be."

She settled for glaring at him before she went up to her room.

She had only a single pair of jeans. She'd brought them in case it was necessary to leave her room at odd hours when she didn't want to get properly dressed—in the early morning to get a newspaper, or something of the sort. Since the Guest House had so far anticipated every one of her wishes, Alex hadn't even bothered to unpack her more casual garb, and she had to take absolutely everything out of her suitcase before she found what she was looking for.

The jeans fit like a second skin; she concluded with regret that she must have put on a pound or two since the last time she'd worn them. But there was no other option, so she held her breath and tugged up the zipper. She added a tailored fuchsia blouse and tied the shirttails at her waist, pushed her feet into tennis shoes and knotted a bright scarf at her throat. Then she slung her handbag over her shoulder and hurried down the stairs.

Kane was in the front hall, apparently negotiating lunch with Mrs. Keith. The housekeeper took one look at Alex, then smiled and murmured, "Oh, yes, I think I know exactly what you mean, sir," and hurried off toward the kitchen.

Kane turned to watch as Alex came down the stairs. One of his dark eyebrows was slightly raised, and his unsmiling regard made her nervous.

"You ordered lunch, so you're going to carry it, that's all I've got to say," Alex told him. "We could live for a week on what she packs for one meal. If I didn't know better, I'd say Mrs. Keith studied with my father... Why are you looking at me like that?"

He walked slowly around her. "Do you happen to have a hairbrush I can borrow?" He gestured toward her pouchlike handbag.

"I don't generally lend my personal—"

"Good."

Alex twisted her head in sudden suspicion, but she was too late; his darting fingers had already tugged the first couple of hairpins out of her smooth French twist, and within seconds the whole mass of shiny black hair was loose around her shoulders. She sighed and dug out the brush. Kane took it out of her hand, ignoring her protests, and wielded it gently until the unruly tresses were subdued. Then he took the scarf from around her throat and used it to tie a ponytail at the nape of her neck.

"There," he said finally. "Doesn't that look better, Mrs. Keith?"

The housekeeper set a basket on the hall table. "Much more casual, I'd say."

"And prettier, too," Kane said. He dropped the brush back into Alex's bag. "You won't need this," he said, easing the strap off her shoulder. "Too much to carry and too tempting to leave in the car, so you might as well put it back in your room. What's this?" He pulled a bright-colored publication out of the side pocket of the bag.

"It's reading material, in case you trek off down the shore and I want to sit still. At least that way I've got something to do."

Kane flipped through the pages. "This isn't even a magazine, Alex. It's a catalog. Dresses and suits and jackets for sale."

"How very observant of you!"

"You read catalogs for fun?"

"Not exactly. I never seem to have time to shop, so when I go on a trip I always take along the catalogs that have come in the mail, and in odd moments I order what I need. That way it's waiting for me when I get home."

"Dump your catalog," Kane said. "If I go off down the beach and leave you sitting on the sand, you can look at the water and think. That's a useful activity, too."

Alex glared at him.

Mrs. Keith offered quietly, "I'll put the things in your room, Miss Jacobi, so you won't have to worry about them."

Kane gave her a sunny smile. "What a wonderful idea. Give her the hairpins, too, Alex."

It didn't matter, Alex told herself. No one was going to see her out there on the beach, and if restyling her hair and banning her possessions made Kane feel powerful, well, that might be useful. After all, half the art of negotiating was to figure out what wasn't important so one could give it up gracefully in order to get something that was.

She handed over the fistful of hairpins, the handbag and the catalog. "I feel absolutely naked," she muttered as they crossed the parking lot to the Ferrari.

Kane let his gaze run over her from ponytail to toes. "If that's your definition of naked, I'll bet you sleep in a long flannel nightie," he speculated.

"I do not care to discuss it, Kane."

"Or maybe fuzzy jammies with feet in them. You'd be cute in a pair of pink bunny pajamas—"

"I only meant I don't as a rule go anywhere without a handbag. Not that I would expect you to understand that."

Kane only grinned.

Alex had the distinct sensation that she was losing all control. "Never mind." She absentmindedly reached for her sunglasses and howled when her hand encountered only air. "I knew I shouldn't have let you take my purse!"

Kane reached into the back of the car and handed her a pair of glasses. Alex studied the odd-shaped pink lenses for a moment and then put the glasses on. "What are these supposed to be?"

"Didn't you ever study geography? Each lens is the shape of Lake Superior."

"How fitting. Do you buy them by the gross for visitors?"

"No, that pair just turned up in the back of the car. I can't think how they got there."

Alex remembered the telltale creak she'd heard during that first telephone conversation and sniffed. She settled back into the low seat and tried to keep track of where they were going. But she had long since lost all sense of direction by the time Kane pulled the Ferrari off the main highway onto a narrow, winding country road.

Alex sat up suspiciously. "This doesn't look like lake country," she accused as the shadow of a pine forest engulfed the car.

"No, it doesn't, but the shore is just over there." Kane pointed. "You'd hear the waves if it weren't for the engine noise." He swung the car off the road into a shady nook. "Come on, I'll show you."

They climbed a ridge, and there was the lake—a very different sight from what Alex had expected. Here, the water was a brilliant blue and almost placid, the waves lapping lazily against a sandy beach.

"It's so dark," she said, drawing a line in the sand with her sneakered toe. "The sand, I mean. It's almost black in places."

"That's because of the iron in it." Kane sat down on an enormous log that had washed high up on the shore and took off his shoes. "Live a little, Alex. The beach is clean."

"I'm sure you'd know." She reluctantly took off her shoes and wriggled her toes in the sand. "What's next?"

Kane took her hands and hauled her to her feet. Then he picked up her shoes, tied the laces together and draped them around her neck. "We walk," he said, and led her down to the water's edge. "And we look."

The sand was warm, but the waves were shockingly cold against her toes, and Alex pulled back in surprise. "And to think I packed a swimsuit," she muttered.

"Only about one week of the year is really fit for swimming," Kane agreed. "The rest of the time we use the health clubs. Except for the real diehards—members of the Polar Bear Club, for instance. They break the ice on New Year's Day and go for a plunge just for the fun of it. It puts a little excitement into an otherwise dull life."

Alex shivered. "I think I could find other forms of entertainment."

"Like polishing up another will? Don't you get tired of estates and trusts? Half the time you're dealing with dead clients."

"At least they don't argue much."

"I'm serious, Alex."

In fact, he sounded almost somber, Alex thought. She nodded. "Yes, sometimes I do get tired of it. It's so very detailed and there isn't a lot of drama. Some days I think about making a change."

"What kind of change?"

"Oh . . . I don't know." She laughed a little, purposely trying to keep the subject casual. "Do you think I've got the stuff to join your negotiating team?"

Kane shook his head. "Not my team."

For a moment she was hurt. He had seemed to like her work just fine once. Then she realized he hadn't meant it that way at all. He'd meant that he wasn't, at the moment, part of *any* team at Pence Whitfield.

"That wasn't a trick question, you know," Alex said. "I wasn't trying to maneuver you into admitting you're dying to come home. I was serious. Do you think I've got the necessary talent to get into your field?''

Kane smiled. ''One more person who's after my job? For shame, Alex.'' He stooped. ''Look, here's an agate.'' He plucked a stone from the mass of pebbles at the water's edge, rinsed it in the next wave and dropped it into Alex's hand.

''There are masses of them here,'' he added. ''Not large, and usually not valuable, but interesting.'' He picked up three more in the next few seconds.

Alex studied the stones and looked down at the sand. She couldn't see anything unusual at all. Then a brilliant white pebble caught her eye, and she stooped to retrieve it.

''That's glass,'' Kane said. ''It's milky because of long exposure to sunlight, and the edges have been rounded by the pounding of the water.''

''It's still pretty,'' Alex said stubbornly. She dropped it into her pocket, along with his agates.

They worked their way down the beach slowly, and her pockets were bulging with pretty stones by the time they came to a mass of huge, irregular dark boulders. The pile of rock, far higher than Alex's head, stretched from water to woods and blocked the way completely. She actually felt disappointed, for on the other side she could see a long stretch of beach. She sighed at its inaccessibility. ''You're right, Kane, this was kind of fun.''

''You're giving up? What's stopping you?'' Sure-footed as a mountain goat, he climbed atop the first boulder and stretched a hand down to her. ''Once we get across this bit, it's really good driftwood pickings.''

''Climb across that pile of rock? You're kidding.''

"Why? These boulders have been here for thousands of years. They aren't going to move and dump you into the lake today."

"I think I'll stay here."

Kane shrugged. "Suit yourself, then. I'm going on."

She sat on the sand for a couple of minutes and watched as he worked his way over the boulders. It didn't look difficult, she found herself thinking. And since she didn't have anything better to do...

It wasn't a difficult climb, but it was tiring. The dark gray boulders were hot against the tender soles of her feet, and the easiest path seemed to lead constantly upward. Finally she sat down to catch her breath and cool her feet, and she watched in fascination as the waves slapped against the rocks. Each burst of water foamed as it struck them, and the impact formed rings of wavelets going back out from shore. There were so many wavelets that a few feet out, the surface looked like a textured plaid blanket.

"You decided to try it, I see," Kane said. He dropped to the rock beside her. "It's nice and warm up here, isn't it? Slate is a wonderful solar collector." He stared out at the horizon.

Alex leaned back against the rock. Whatever force had arranged these blocks millennia ago, it had very kindly left a curving surface that fit her body perfectly. The warmth soaked into her bones. She started to yawn, then tried to hide it as Kane turned to look quizzically at her.

"I'm not bored," she protested. "It's just..."

Kane nodded. "The lake effect. The sound of water drains all the tension away."

They sat there in peaceful silence for long minutes. The only sounds were the call of gulls, the softly hypnotic splash of the waves and the delighted shriek of a child far down the beach.

They might have been alone in paradise, Alex thought.

"I've always thought that Eden should have been a beach and not a garden," Kane murmured.

She looked at him with wide-eyed surprise.

"Sorry to shock you. That's an irreverent thought, I know." He stared out to sea, eyes narrowed against the glare on the water.

"No. Not at all. I mean, I was thinking almost the same thing."

Kane turned his head slowly. "Were you? Did you read my mind, I wonder—or did I read yours?"

He was going to kiss her; she could see the intention in his eyes. "I don't know," she said hastily. "I . . ."

But apparently Kane was not interested in the answer. He leaned over and his mouth brushed hers, softly at first and then with increasing sureness.

Alex's insides felt like jelly in an earthquake. The sense that she was about to tumble off the edge of the world was overwhelming; it took every bit of self-control she possessed not to desperately grab hold of Kane to keep herself from falling. And when he finally raised his head and Alex opened her eyes, the sky seemed to be revolving above her, so she shut them again for a while.

Neither of them said anything. Eventually the whirling stopped and Alex sat up, her arms wrapped around her knees, and stared out at the lake.

Kane said without looking at her, "If you're waiting for me to apologize, don't plan on it being any time soon. I've wanted to do that since that silly Christmas party."

Alex sucked in a startled breath. The air jammed in her throat and she started to cough.

"If I had," Kane mused, "you'd have sued me and Pence Whitfield for sexual harassment, I suppose. But now that we're not colleagues anymore . . . no, I'm not going to say I'm sorry."

Alex tried out a dozen different answers in her head. They all sounded prudish or defensive, even stupid. And after all, the man had stolen a kiss—not exactly a terrible offense. And it was a great kiss.

She cleared her throat and said, "Why do you keep insisting you're not coming back to Pence Whitfield, Kane?"

For several aeons-long seconds she thought he wasn't going to answer. Finally he said very quietly, "Because I'm not, Alexandra."

He sounded absolutely serious, she thought. And perhaps at the moment he really believed it. "That's some case of burnout you've got," she murmured. "You've been at Pence Whitfield five years, right?"

"Just about."

"And you've been on the mergers-and-acquisitions team all that time?"

He nodded.

"Well, it's no wonder you're tired." She waited for an answer, and when none was forthcoming she tried again. "Do you mind telling me what you plan to do, instead?"

Humor flashed in his eyes. "I understand you could use another secretary."

Alex put a hand on his wrist. "Kane, if you say you're not coming back, all right, I'll do my best to take you seriously. But you have to give me the same respect. You owe me an explanation."

Kane sobered abruptly. He looked down at her hand, pale against his tanned wrist, and the fingertips of his other hand came to rest on her knuckles.

The contact tingled, as if an electrical charge was running through his hand and into hers. "I want to know why, Kane."

"Too many long days, too much work, not enough time."

Alex tried to keep her voice even and noncommittal. "That's the modern complaint. It's the price of success."

Kane shook his head. "It's too high a price. You know, for a while I thought the money made everything worthwhile, but—"

He stopped, and after patiently waiting a while Alex decided he wasn't going to say any more. "The money's nice, you have to admit," she pointed out. "Pence Whitfield is very generous."

"Money isn't everything, Alex. It can't buy time."

She couldn't help feeling annoyed. "That's such a cliché, Kane! Time isn't worth all that much, either, if it isn't well used. Of course it's fun to walk on the beach now and then, but if you did it every day, you'd soon get pretty bored. If you aren't doing something worthwhile with your time—"

"Like making money? We seem to have come full circle."

Alex was silent.

When he finally spoke again, Kane's voice was so soft she had to strain to hear. "I saw Aunt Tess twice during the last year of her life. I live less than three hours away, but I saw her only twice."

Alex put a hand out to him again. "You can't blame yourself for that, Kane. It's unfortunate, and of course it hurt. But how were you to know it was the last chance you'd have?''

He pulled away and turned to face her. "That's my point exactly. I knew she was ill. But even if I hadn't known, I certainly understood she wasn't going to live forever. The woman was well into her seventies, Alex. But I didn't make time to visit her more often.''

"Feeling guilty about it isn't going to help now, Kane.''

He pulled away from her gentle touch, and frustration filled his voice. "It isn't just that. Don't you understand? It made me reassess my whole life. How do any of us know how much time we have? I could work like hell for twenty years and die the night before I was to retire and enjoy all the wealth I'd accumulated.''

"Well,'' Alex said crisply, "if you're going to look at it that way, any of us could die at any time.''

"That's exactly right. And I'd much rather die doing something I like. Wouldn't you?''

"Beachcombing?''

"If that's what I want to do, why shouldn't I?''

Alex sighed and leaned back against the warm rock. "So what happens if you don't die? What are you going to live on? You've gotten used to a pretty high standard of living the past few years.''

"You do have money on the brain, don't you, Alex?''

She jerked upright again. "I don't know what kind of family you grew up in, Kane Forrestal. But I'll bet you never had to worry where your next baseball glove came from, much less the things you really needed. So before you look down your nose at me, you might remember that not everyone was fortunate enough to grow up in the upper class—''

"I didn't.''

"Or even in the middle. We were darned near dirt-poor when I was a kid. There were weeks when there wasn't any money in the till to pay the suppliers and no certainty that there would be any time soon. Of course I want more security than that. And if I can get it by doing something I love, why shouldn't I go right on doing it?"

"That's the difference between us," he said. "You see, I don't love it anymore."

There was a note of hopelessness in his voice that touched Alex's heart. He really did feel his career was over. How on earth could she convince him otherwise? If he would just wait awhile, have a rest, things would look brighter, she was certain. "Even a bad case of burnout can heal, Kane," she said gently. "Take some time off."

"Good advice. I plan to do just that. Lots of time." He pushed himself up from the rocks. "There's a piece of driftwood down there I want."

Obviously, Alex thought, the subject was closed. She had accomplished nothing; in fact, she had probably destroyed any chance he might talk to her seriously again.

But at least she now knew what she was dealing with, she told herself stoutly. Wasn't that progress, of a sort?

CHAPTER SIX

ALEX'S HEART CREPT into her throat at the way Kane crossed the boulders. He wasn't picking his way, he was simply walking, scarcely pausing to test a foothold before putting his weight on it. When he bent to reach for the bit of wood that was his objective, Alex's face paled. He wasn't even hanging on to any supports; he had both hands on the wood, trying to pull it loose from the rocks where it was wedged. A good ten feet below him was the lake, and there was nothing but slate boulders to break his fall if he slipped.

He was back on relatively safe rock waving his prize before Alex realized she'd been clenching her hands so hard she'd cut ridges into her palms. She uncurled her fists and told herself wryly that if he broke his fool neck, at least he'd die happy, doing what he loved. Wasn't that what he'd said he wanted?

The piece of driftwood turned out to be a long, skinny, gnarled branch of a tree, bleached to gray by the sun and polished almost smooth by the action of the waves.

Kane held it out to her. "Let's get a measurement."

"Of what?"

"The proper height for a walking stick for you. This is a perfect one. The knot in the top makes a wonderful knob to grip, and once we cut it off at the right length..."

"I can just see myself strolling through the skywalks with it," Alex agreed.

Kane smiled. "It'll come in handy when you don't agree with a judge's ruling, too."

The playful note was back in his voice. It was as much a warning to stay off the subject of his career as plastering a sign across his chest, and Alex smothered the urge to shake him. She would just have to be patient and look for another way to approach the problem, that was all. She wasn't about to give up.

He took her back to the Guest House in midafternoon, saying vaguely that he had some things to do. Alex had to bite her tongue to keep from asking what. It was none of her business, after all, whether his Saturday-night entertainment was blond, brunette or redheaded.

As she showered she considered her options for the rest of the day. She could go back to the warehouse; there was certainly enough to do there to keep her busy for hours. But the prospect of coming out of that silent isolated building after dark was unappealing.

She could work on her progress report. The trouble was she hadn't made enough progress in the past twenty-four hours to be worth reporting.

So she called Joanna Adler's hospital room and got an update on what, by all accounts, was the world's most adorable baby. Then, purely on a whim, Alex picked up the pink-and-blue quilt and went downstairs to sit on the patio that ran the entire length of the back of the Guest House.

Her deep-cushioned deck chair was so comfortable and the rhythmic pattern of her stitches so soothing that she wasn't aware of the desk clerk's approach. "Miss Jacobi, a Mr. Wintergreen is on the phone for you."

Alex wondered vaguely how Geoffrey had managed to find a pay phone in heaven and realized abruptly that she must have dozed off. Her hand was cramped because she was still clutching the quilt, the needle already set in the next stitch. She flexed her fingers carefully, feeling as if the knuckles were likely to break, as she went inside to the little walnut-lined telephone booth beneath the Guest House stairs.

"Hello, Paul," she said. Her voice came out lower than usual, and more sultry.

There was a sniff at the other end of the line. "I should have known Paul would have a siren for an attorney."

The voice was harsh and nasal, as different from Paul's intimate softness as it was possible to get. Alex put two fingertips to the center of her forehead, where a small throbbing pain had suddenly developed. "You must be Ralph Wintergreen."

"Congratulations. I'd like to talk to you."

Alex said cautiously, "That could be arranged, I'm sure. I'll be here for a few—"

"How about tonight? Or has cousin Paul got you sewed up for a date?"

"I happen to be free this evening." Alex's tone was icy.

"There's a coffee chop in Lakeside, not far from where you are." He gave the address. "I'll meet you there in an hour."

"With your attorney?"

"I don't have an attorney, Miss Jacobi. That's why I want to talk to you—to find out if I'm going to need one."

The line went dead. Alex shifted uneasily on the little wrought-iron stool in the telephone booth. There was nothing wrong with talking to him, she assured herself. There would be no conflict of interest unless Ralph Wintergreen actually filed a suit contesting the will; until that time, Alex technically represented him, as well as Paul, since both were beneficiaries of Geoffrey's estate.

Still, the situation called for caution. A possible plaintiff asking to talk to the defense's attorney. What was Ralph Wintergreen up to, anyway? Should she call Kane for advice? She certainly wouldn't mind having his opinion on the matter; he knew more about Ralph than she did. On the other hand, considering what Kane had told her today, she didn't think he'd be flattered by the request for help. He'd probably see it simply as a ploy to get him involved in the law again.

Alex straightened her spine stubbornly and decided that she wouldn't give him the opportunity to accuse her of manipulating him. She could handle this by herself. Kane had once told her she was a perfectly competent attorney. And she was.

Besides, she thought as she stood in front of her mirror and added a touch of eye shadow and mascara, there was simply no reason for her to feel this suspicious of Ralph Wintergreen. The man wanted to talk, that was all. It wasn't as though he was a convicted felon. He'd made no threats, and he hadn't proposed meeting in some sleazy bar along the waterfront. There was no reason to think this would be different from any other chat with a client.

Still, she made sure the desk clerk knew where she was going, just in case.

THE GUEST HOUSE promised continental breakfast every day, but on Sundays, Alex found, it wasn't so much a meal as a banquet. She gasped when she saw the tray and then scrambled to clear enough space on the low table by the couch for the bellboy to set it down.

After he left she simply stood for a moment staring at the spread. There was a full thermos of coffee, a carafe of juice, a basket of assorted rolls and muffins, and a bowl of fruit—plenty of food, she thought, for two people with enormous appetites or a whole monastery of ascetics. And the Sunday newspaper was neatly folded on a corner of the tray, providing entertainment—or perhaps "temptation" was a better word—for the entire morning.

She had just poured her coffee when there was a knock on the door. Alex tightened the belt of her robe and padded over to answer it.

Mrs. Keith held out a fresh smelling pile of clean clothes—Alex's jeans, the fuchsia blouse, even her scarf, which had seemed last night to have sand permanently embedded between the fibers.

"You are a wonder!" Alex exclaimed.

"Just part of the service. You haven't touched your tray, dear. Is there anything wrong?"

"Not at all. I'm debating where to start. It's a waste to send me so much food, you know."

"I thought perhaps you'd want to invite a guest." The housekeeper smiled. "If you'd like another cup sent up, just let me know."

"Not a bad idea," Alex murmured as she sank onto the couch again. She'd call Kane and ask him to breakfast. And if during the course of the morning the conversation worked its way round to Ralph Wintergreen and the chat she'd had with him last night...

It was barely nine in the morning, but there was no answer at Inglenook. Either Kane hadn't yet come home from the night before, or he'd unplugged the phone.

In either case, Alex decided, it wasn't going to bother her. She didn't need him, anyway.

She thoughtfully munched on a croissant while she read the news section of the paper, and as soon as the mantel clock struck ten she dialed Pence Whitfield's main number. Alex wasn't surprised when the telephone was answered on the second ring. No answering services for Pence Whitfield; the weekend receptionists—and for that matter, the midnight ones—were just as professional as the everyday crew. And as usual on Sunday morning, Neville Morgan was in his office. That was one of the things Alex liked best about the firm; the partners were almost always available for consultation.

"Alexandra," he said with cheerful satisfaction. "What can I do for you?"

"It's the Wintergreen case, Mr. Morgan. You'll have my updated report tomorrow, but last night something very strange happened, and I wanted to talk it over with you before I put it on paper."

"Strange? What do you mean?" There was a rustle of documents in the background.

"Ralph Wintergreen called and wanted to meet with me. So we met and had quite a long talk, but the main message was that if he decides to sue over the estate, it'll be a nasty and embarrassing battle for Paul."

"Threats," Neville Morgan said dismissively. "Meaningless threats. Every troublemaker says things like that. You'll get attuned to it soon enough."

Alex was shaking her head. "I don't think it *was* a threat, Mr. Morgan. It sounded more like a guarantee. He said—"

"Relax, Alexandra. It's just a bluff, and you fell for it. Of course he wants us worried and defensive, because if we panic and negotiate a settlement, he can walk away clear without ever having to prove a thing. I'll bet the fact is he can't."

"Well, I haven't come across anything compromising yet in Geoffrey's papers, but—"

"And I don't think you will. Geoffrey made very clear what he wanted, and I wrote it precisely that way." He cleared his throat. "No, I think we're invincible on the will, no matter how much Ralph blusters. Don't panic over it, Alexandra." He paused, then, "How's Kane?"

Alex said cautiously, "He seems to be just fine."

Neville Morgan chuckled. "I didn't think you were likely to find him depressed and suicidal over the Quadrangle affair."

"Hardly. But he's got a terrible case of burnout, I'm afraid."

Neville Morgan's voice was cool. "Is that his diagnosis or yours?"

"He told me all the fun has gone out of law for him."

"Well, burnout is certainly a fine catchall phrase, wouldn't you say? It fits all kinds of symptoms—or none at all."

Alex bit her tongue, hard. It wasn't fair to expect Neville Morgan to understand. He hadn't seen Kane yesterday, she reminded herself. He hadn't heard Kane's voice when he said, "I don't love it anymore." The gloom in Kane's tone had not been manufactured.

"And even if you're right," Neville Morgan went on blithely, "burnout doesn't last. He'll soon be so bored he can't see straight. We'll just have to put things off a while longer at this end, I suppose, and let him work it out. But I can't emphasize enough how much we're depending on you, Alexandra."

"Thanks for the confidence," she muttered after she'd put the phone down. "Even if it is misplaced. I'm the first team, and I can't even *find* the man today, much less make a dent in his determination."

She allowed herself exactly two minutes to feel sorry for herself and then made her regular call to Jacobi's.

When she was in the city, she paid Gus a visit every Sunday; when she was traveling, she always tried to find a few minutes to call him.

This time she was hardly past a greeting when Gus demanded to know what was wrong.

Alex was puzzled. "Nothing, Papa."

"Something's not right. I can hear it in your voice. Are you eating enough?"

Alex surveyed the almost-untouched breakfast tray and sighed. "You should see the way they're feeding me. Caramel rolls and croissants and French bread and—"

Gus snorted. "Lots of starch. How about tucking into some good old bacon and eggs? Put some real fuel into you, and you'll soon have the sparkle back in those eyes."

Alex had to laugh. "It's not the food, Papa. The job's going slowly, and that's frustrating, but—"

"When will you be home?"

When Kane comes back down to earth, she thought. Which, at the present rate, might be sometime after the turn of the century. "I don't know. You should see the stacks of paper I have to get through."

"Paper shouldn't bother you. It's just like homework, and there's always something else worth learning."

"I'll try to look at it that way."

Gus clucked his tongue. "For shame, Alex. Think of the opportunity you've got, and you don't appreciate it."

"Maybe you should have tied an apron on me and made me wash dishes now and then, Papa."

"Don't see why. You can't learn anything with your hands in hot water."

It was his standard answer, given so often over the years she was certain he no longer thought about it. Alex did, though, after she said goodbye.

"You can't learn anything with your hands in hot water." Gus was wrong, she thought. There *was* something to be learned. People could discover that they hated washing dishes and that the disadvantages of another kind of job paled in comparison.

She wondered if that lesson applied to Kane. Certainly the pressure at Pence Whitfield added a difficult side to the practice of law, but it was unavoidable, what with the kind and number of cases the firm handled. Kane didn't seem to realize he was throwing away a great deal of good in order to eliminate that pressure. How on earth could she make him see what he was sacrificing before it was too late?

ALEX SPENT A COUPLE of hours at the warehouse that afternoon. She actually found herself enjoying a prolonged exchange of letters between Geoffrey and a landscape architect who had been hired to revamp the gardens on the Wintergreen family estate. At first glance it was an acrimonious debate, but Alex sensed that underneath the razor sharpness of Geoffrey's comments, the old guy had been enjoying himself. It was almost as if he'd found a game that was more fun than chess by mail, she reflected. And it lasted longer, too; the correspondence over the garden had gone on for nearly a year. Geoffrey had won in the end, of course. Apparently he always came out ahead.

She worked longer than she'd planned, partly to see whether the garden debate had ended with a bang or trickled off into nothing. When she came out of the warehouse, the sun was setting. On a whim, she turned away from the lake looking for a better view of the western sky. The city clung to a series of steep hills, and she finally found her way to the top of one just in time to admire the last fading streaks of violet and pink and silver.

It was questionable whether the effort had been worth it, however, because she ended up so thoroughly lost that if it hadn't been for the glimpse of the lake in the distance, she wouldn't have had any idea of where she was at all. By the time she found her way back to the lakeshore, she'd missed the Guest House altogether and was on the scenic highway that led out to Inglenook. She almost turned back before she realized she might as well put her confusion to good use and drop in on Kane.

The Ferrari was parked in the drive, its For Sale sign clearly visible to any passing car. Every window in the house was open to the cool evening air. Alex didn't see the mountain bike propped up next to the back door until she was almost beside it, and in the same moment she heard a feminine voice—low and soft—from the kitchen.

But it was too late to back out; the sound of her footsteps on the elevated deck must have been audible to the people inside. So she tapped on the door. "Kane?"

He held it open silently and she stepped into the kitchen.

"Sorry," Alex said. "I know I should have called. But the truth is I just got myself lost again and I was so frazzled—and so happy once I realized where I was—that I thought you might give me a cup of coffee..."

Alex's voice trailed off as she got a good look at the woman standing beside the small breakfast table wristdeep in soft black soil as she efficiently settled a houseplant into a new pot. Her face was soft and pink and mapped with lines, and her hair was silvery gray.

"That's enough for today," the woman said, as she dusted off her hands. "One more session and I'll be finished. I'll need some more potting soil, though."

I've heard that voice, Alex thought. *In the background of that telephone conversation.*

The woman moved across the kitchen to put the plastic bag of potting soil away in the cabinet beneath the sink. The door creaked.

And I've heard that sound, too, Alex thought. So he wasn't in bed with a woman that afternoon; he was getting his houseplants repotted!

"Since Kane doesn't seem to be inclined to introductions," the woman said as she scrubbed her hands, "shall we take care of it ourselves? You're Alexandra Jacobi, I'll bet. I'm Fiona James. Kane's aunt Tess was my best friend."

Alex held out her hand. "And you like to spoil him a bit?" she guessed.

"Oh, I'm not doing this for him," Fiona assured her. "It's just that Tess would haunt the place if Kane let her hibiscus die." She nodded toward the glossy-leafed plant on the table.

Alex reached out tentatively to touch a brilliant red flower. It looked as if it was made of crepe paper, but it was softer. "It's beautiful. And it looks perfectly healthy."

"Root-bound," Fiona said succinctly. "Otherwise I wouldn't dream of repotting it now, in this season. I'd better be going, Kane, before it's completely dark. Don't forget to buy another bag of soil so I can do the sansevieria next time." She let the door slam behind her, and a moment later the mountain bike rolled out of sight down the scenic highway.

"You got lost again?" Kane asked. There was a note of doubt in his voice.

Alex lifted her chin stubbornly. She might have exaggerated, but she wasn't lying. What did he think she was doing, anyway? Spying on him? "It's ridiculous, isn't it? I can find my way around cities of millions. I've never been confused by the New York subway. Why should Duluth absolutely confound me?"

He smiled a little. "Don't you know?"

"It's an impossible town?" Alex hazarded.

"It's a threat to your peace of mind, Alex."

"You can say that again." She touched the hibiscus bloom once more. "This is beautiful. I wish I could have flowers at home."

"Why can't you?"

"I don't have a Fiona to look after them for me. Who would water them this week, for instance, while I'm gone?"

Kane shrugged. "We all make choices, I suppose. Want to go for a walk?"

She didn't hesitate. "Sure."

He picked up a flashlight, but he didn't bother to close the windows or lock the door. At the end of the drive he paused and glanced at Alex. "Which way do you . . . No, perhaps I'd better stay in control of the expedition. We could end up in Arizona with you in charge."

Alex bit her tongue and said nothing.

The light was fading, but the shoulders of the road were wide and even, and Kane's flashlight and white sweater would make them visible to any traffic. They walked for a few minutes in silence, and then Kane mused, "Maybe I'll trade in the hibiscus for a dog."

"Why on earth would you want a dog?" That would be worse than plants, she thought. Who would take care of an animal when Kane wasn't able to?

"For companionship and adoration. So I'll always have someone around who wants to go for a walk."

Alex stopped. "Wait a minute. If you dare tell me to heel, I'll . . . I'll bite you."

He smiled. "And dogs don't talk back, either." He pointed out at the lake. "Look at the loon. He's fishing for a late supper."

Alex sat down on a railing at the roadside and watched as the strange-looking bird bent his head one way, then the other, as if listening. Abruptly he tipped head down and vanished beneath the waves. She was beginning to think the loon had disappeared forever when he showed up again, fifty feet farther from shore, bobbing contentedly in the rolling waves.

"Kane," she said slowly, "why are you so certain Geoffrey Wintergreen told Ralph—or at least let him believe—that he'd get a full share?"

Kane drew her to her feet and tucked her hand into the bend of his elbow. "It sounds as if you're beginning to have doubts about it yourself," he said.

"Ralph called me last night. In fact, I spent most of the evening with him. And after I listened to him . . . Ralph is brusque and cynical and dry and funny, just like Geoffrey."

"So you're getting to know the old guy, after all, are you?"

"You were right about that. As I read his letters I can almost hear him talking. And I imagine he liked Ralph."

For some time the road had been quiet, deserted, with no buildings in sight. Now, as they rounded a bend, a small commercial development came into view up ahead.

"There's a little bar at that motel," Kane said. "How about a cold drink?"

Alex shivered. "I'd much rather have a hot one."

The bar was well-lit, clean and quiet, with only half a dozen patrons. They took a corner booth, and Alex ordered coffee. She wrapped her hands around the big stoneware mug and let the heat soak into her fingers, and watched as Kane stirred the whipped cream into his hot chocolate.

"I just can't explain why Geoffrey's will didn't reflect his liking for Ralph, if he really felt that way," she said slowly. "He should have had ample time to change it."

"What suddenly convinced you that Ralph's telling the truth?"

Alex let her lashes drop to hide the hint of triumph in her eyes. He couldn't stay out of a good legal question for long, could he? "I didn't say I believed him exactly," she pointed out. "He assured me he can prove his claim, but he wouldn't show me the evidence."

"What evidence? A letter?"

"He wouldn't say. Neville Morgan says it's all a bluff, of course." She propped her elbows on the table, her mug cradled in both hands. "You haven't answered my question, Kane. Why do you believe Ralph?"

"I'm not sure Geoffrey had a great opinion of Ralph. But I don't think he was all that fond of Paul, either. I'd have expected him to treat them equally badly." He shrugged. "Sorry to disappoint you, Alex. Just a human hunch, that's all—nothing admissible in court."

"And I'm supposed to believe you've forgotten everything you ever knew about legal reasoning now that you've retired?" Alex said dryly.

Kane smiled a little.

She was annoyed by that careless little lift of the corners of his mouth, and she set her mug down with a thump. Coffee slopped over the rim and the heat stung her hand, but she hardly noticed. "How can you just turn your back on your profession?" she demanded. "How can you throw away what you've worked so hard for?"

Kane reached for a paper napkin and began to blot up the mess. "Alex—"

"All right, you've got what looks like the world's worst case of burnout. After the Quadrangle mess, it's no wonder."

"Quadrangle was no messier than most of my cases," Kane pointed out. "It just came out differently."

Alex was in no mood to argue about details. "But this horrible dissatisfaction will pass, Kane. Maybe you do need a couple of months to recuperate, but don't throw your career away over it!"

He hadn't finished mopping up the table, but he paused, the soggy paper napkin still in his hand. "So you're convinced all I need is a rest? You just don't listen, do you, Alex?"

She threw out one hand in a gesture of disgust. "All right," she said. "So you carry out this threat to quit. What are you doing to do, instead? Be the voice of doom on a network-news show?"

Kane put the dripping napkin neatly into an ashtray. "That's a possibility," he said thoughtfully. "I'd be a great news anchor."

He had something there, Alex thought. She could picture Kane as a steadying force in a gale, a rock to cling to. An anchor.

At least, she told herself, once upon a time he'd been all those things. Before he'd gone completely berserk.

"I think I should go home," she said.

She waited by the door, looking out toward the lake, as he paid their bill. It was completely dark now, and the people coming into the motel complex were wearing jackets and sweaters. It was going to be a long walk back to Inglenook, Alex thought.

Kane saw her shiver. "Come on. I think the gift shop is still open."

She couldn't quite see what difference that made until he guided her into a tiny glass-walled nook off the lobby and over to a rack of sweatshirts. "They carry everything for the unprepared tourist," he said as he flipped through the hangers.

"They must sell thousands of these to unsuspecting people who come up here thinking beaches mean sunbathing."

Kane tugged a sweatshirt off the hanger. "Here. This is perfect."

Alex took it without enthusiasm. It was white, with some kind of shield or seal printed on the front in bright red. "Is it the right size?"

"It doesn't matter with sweatshirts."

She eyed him, and then the label. "Extra large?"

"That's about right."

She couldn't decide whether to kick him or weep. "You think I'm an extra large, Kane?"

"You'll be warmer that way. The bigger the better, because there's more air trapped underneath for insulation."

"In that case, I'll take it."

"It's my gift," Kane said smoothly. "Just a souvenir of Duluth." He handed the shirt to the clerk, and as the young man folded it, Alex saw the shield clearly for the first time.

"Official Great Lakes Navigator," it read, around what looked like an actual Coast Guard crest.

Kane pulled out his wallet. "Do you have a laundry marker?" he asked the clerk. "I'll pay extra if you can draw a question mark after that title."

Alex punched him in the arm.

He grinned and helped her pull the sweatshirt over her head.

He was right, Alex thought as they walked back toward Inglenook. The oversize sweatshirt was fleecy and warm. And his hand holding hers didn't hurt her comfort level, either.

She didn't want to talk. She just wanted to walk along beside him in the cool darkness and enjoy the rhythm of their steps and the way their clasped hands swung easily. But the disagreement that lay between them was too big for her to remain silent.

"Every job has its problems," she began almost tentatively. "And you're so good at the law, Kane. To see you throw away everything you've built for yourself at Pence Whitfield just breaks my heart." She counted off ten steps and added quietly, "What would it take to make it worthwhile again?"

After long seconds he said quietly, "You're talking about things like corner offices and limousines and club memberships and private planes?"

"Maybe. Whatever you want. Not that I can promise anything," she added quickly, "but—"

"Don't you ever ask yourself what it's worth, Alex?"

She shook her head in puzzlement. "Of course not. It's hard work, yes, but it's worth it. Someday I'll be a partner. That's what I've always wanted and worked for, and I can do it."

"Funny," he mused. "One of the last bits of advice Aunt Tess gave me was, 'Do what you should do, not necessarily what you're capable of.'"

Alex was so absorbed she would have walked right past Inglenook if Kane hadn't stopped at the end of the driveway.

"I don't understand that," she admitted.

He sighed. "I know you don't."

But he made no move to explain. Finally she said, "Thanks for the walk, Kane. And the coffee. And the sweatshirt." She paused. "And the talk."

"Even if you don't understand," he added softly. He bent his head and kissed her, slowly and thoroughly.

And, somehow, the kiss was very sad, too, Alex thought. She almost stumbled as she turned toward her car.

"Oh, Alex?"

She wheeled around eagerly, expecting him to explain Aunt Tess and her cryptic comment, after all.

"Just keep the lake on your left," Kane said, "so you won't get lost on your way home."

CHAPTER SEVEN

Do what you should do, not necessarily what you're capable of...

Aunt Tess's advice to Kane still didn't make any sense to Alex, even after she'd slept on it. Why would Tess not have wanted him to fulfill his potential by doing everything he was capable of doing? It didn't take a psychic to know that the woman had adored Kane. Why wouldn't she have wanted the best for him?

Had she been taking a moral stand on the law? If that was so, Aunt Tess wouldn't have been the only one, Alex thought. Too many laymen didn't understand what the legal system was all about. Many thought that only one side of a case could be right and true, and that any attorney who took the other side was nothing but a shyster. Many people simply didn't understand that no matter how clear the thing looked, it was possible for more than one side of an argument to be equally right, equally true, and therefore the only fair way to make a decision was to consider all the arguments.

If that was the sort of thing Tess had meant, however, why hadn't Kane straightened out the woman's confusion and explained how the legal system really worked? Instead, he seemed to have taken Tess's advice very seriously indeed.

Or was it possible Tess had meant something else altogether? *What you're capable of...* Had she been warning that Kane had a bad side, that he might get caught up in criminal behavior?

Don't be ridiculous, Alex told herself crossly. *He never would have told you what Tess said, if that's what she was talking about.*

She was disgusted with herself for even thinking of such a possibility. Kane as a master criminal. What an absurd notion!

Alex was ready to head to the warehouse, but she was still in her room waiting for a fax line at Pence Whitfield to open up so she could send her progress report to Neville Morgan when the regular telephone rang. The soft feminine voice that greeted Alex startled her. Why on earth was Kane's friend Fiona calling her at all, much less at this hour on a Monday morning?

"What can I do for you, Miss James?" Alex hesitated. "Or is it Mrs. James?"

"Dear heaven, girl, call me Fiona. 'Miss James' makes me sound old enough to be your great-aunt. Which I am, of course, but it's rude of you to remind me of the fact." There was a throaty chuckle. "Kane tells me you're an expert on how to break a will."

Just what I need, Alex thought. Sometimes it seemed that for every will written there was at least one person who felt cheated by the outcome. And usually that person was equally certain that if the right legal trick could be discovered, he or she would end up rich....

Alex sighed and said cautiously, "I specialize in estates and trusts and wills, that's true, but as far as overturning a will goes, I'm afraid it's not all that easy."

"I know," Fiona James said bluntly. "In fact, I'm damned if I can see any way to get this one thrown out. That's why I'm calling you."

Alex frowned and held the receiver a couple of inches away so she could pull off her gold button earring. Maybe that would help, she thought. Something was certainly getting in the way of her hearing. "I'm afraid I don't understand."

"I have a client who got an absolutely raw deal. She came to me, and I had to tell her I thought it was hopeless. But when Kane told me you work with that sort of thing all the time—"

"You're an attorney?"

Fiona chuckled again. "I gather Kane didn't give you any details. Well, I'm sure you had better things to talk about. At any rate, about this client of mine—"

"Miss James...Fiona. I'm sorry, but I really have more than I can handle right now. I couldn't possibly take on another client."

"I'm not exactly offering you a client. For one thing, she couldn't afford to pay your hourly fees," Fiona said frankly.

"You're working on a contingency basis?"

"I'm working on a twenty-dollar retainer at the moment. If you'd like me to split it with you, I'd be happy to, but what I'd really like to get for her is some free advice."

"Fiona, I can't—"

"She's a single mother with a year-old baby. The will in question ties up everything so tightly she's practically starving, and meanwhile the trustee is frittering the money away on frivolous expenses."

Despite herself, Alex was intrigued. "It's the baby's father's will?" she said.

"Nope. Paternal grandfather's. And he didn't disinherit the child, nothing like that. There just won't be anything left by the time the kid turns eighteen."

"There's no way to challenge the trustee?"

"Not that I've found. There's nothing wrong with the mother, by the way, except that Grandpa didn't like her. She'd have made a wonderful trustee herself."

There was a long silence. Alex bit her lip. "I'll take a look. No promises."

"Didn't ask you to make any," Fiona said crisply. "How about six this evening at my office?"

Alex agreed and jotted down the address on the back of her business card. "Just what I need," she muttered as she put the telephone down. "A worthy cause to fill up my last spare half hour a day."

She wondered what Kane would think when he heard about this.

"I DON'T KNOW WHY you should waste your time talking to Geoffrey's old servants," Paul Wintergreen said. He tapped his well-manicured fingertips on the polished surface of the French Provincial desk. "If Ralph says he's got this evidence of his in writing—"

"He didn't say that," Alex reminded him. "He just said he had evidence. He could have meant a letter, or a sworn statement from one of Geoffrey's friends or servants. But it could also be any number of other things—tape recordings, someone's verbal testimony. It wouldn't be very wise of him not to get it in writing, if that's the case, but—"

"Isn't there some way to force him to say what it is?"

"When we get into court proceedings, yes. He'd have to show evidence almost immediately then, or the case would be thrown out. But until then—"

"*If* we get into court, don't you mean? I still say he's bluffing." Paul rose restlessly and crossed to the window.

"You may be right," Alex conceded. "However, I'd be much more comfortable if I knew there were no surprises lurking among the servants."

"Very well, I'll have my secretary run the addresses down for you." Paul smiled wistfully. "Personally I think Ralph is simply taking his revenge this way, by keeping everything in an uproar for heaven knows how long. But, as Neville Morgan says, we can't allow someone like Ralph to toy with the entire system of justice, can we?" He came toward her chair. "How about a drink somewhere, Alexandra? It's time to quit for the day."

Alex checked her watch and rose. "I'm sorry. I have another appointment."

His eyebrows arched haughtily. "I thought you were in Duluth to conduct *my* business."

"Don't worry, Paul," she said with only a whisper of sarcasm. "I won't bill you for the time."

When Alex found her way to the address Fiona James had given her, she was startled by what she found. For a minute she thought she might have written down the number wrong. Then she remembered the twenty-dollar retainer and realized that she shouldn't have been so surprised to find Fiona practicing law in a storefront on the edge of downtown.

She probably has a plant shop in front to help cover expenses, Alex thought as she dug her briefcase out of the back of her car.

But the rooms behind the storefront, though strictly utilitarian, were surprisingly attractive. The decor was quiet, in serene blues and greens. There was no fancy carved wood, no expensive art on the walls, no deep plush carpets, but the furniture hadn't been provided by government surplus, either. A waiting room furnished with comfortable chairs spanned the front of the building; the rest of the floor space was taken up with half a dozen office cubicles, their doors stretching down a long central aisle. It was apparent that everything had been done on a budget, but with no lack of good taste.

The receptionist looked up with a smile. "Hello, Miss Jacobi."

Alex was surprised. "How did you know my name?"

The young woman looked a bit embarrassed. "Oh, we don't get too many clients who are dressed like you. Fiona said she'll be with you as soon as she can."

Alex looked around for a chair.

"I can get the case file," the receptionist offered. "And that first office is available if you'd like to use it."

The room was small and efficiently organized. The desk was well equipped, but there was nothing personal in evidence to hint at whom it might belong to. Alex turned on the desk lamp and spread the manila folder out on the blotter. She leafed through the contents, then settled down to read Fiona's notes on her conversations with her client.

A few minutes later Fiona herself popped her head in. She didn't look much different than she had yesterday in Kane's kitchen, Alex thought. She was wearing tweed trousers and a sweater, and her silvery hair had a flyaway look, as if she'd ridden her bike to work and forgotten to check a mirror when she'd arrived.

"I'm glad you could stop by," Fiona said. "I can't wait to see what you come up with."

"No miracles yet." Alex pushed the folder aside. "We can't haul the trustee into court for violating the restrictions on how he invests the money, since Grandpa foolishly didn't specify any. And I assume he hasn't yet done anything so blindingly obvious that the court would believe he was deliberately wasting money."

Fiona shook her head. "There's just been a string of heavy expenses for the estate," she said darkly. She came in and sat down in the client's chair across the desk from Alex. "At least that's what he says. The list is there."

"I see. There's nothing that leaps out as being exorbitant, but the whole thing does have an aroma of fish, doesn't it?"

"Yes. And I'm afraid he's well aware we can't do anything to touch him."

Alex picked up the will again. It was a thick cumbersome document. "I don't suppose you can prove that some of the money ended up in his best friend's pocket or anything like that?"

Fiona sighed. "I have all kinds of suspicions. But proving it... Well, you know what that kind of investigation costs. Private detectives aren't cheap, and I can't in good conscience urge my client to borrow the money to hire one."

"Unless you're already certain of what he'll find," Alex agreed. "In which case you wouldn't need the investigator—most of your clients can't really afford even you, can they?"

Fiona smiled wryly. "True, here at the clinic we handle a good many clients who fall into the category of the 'working poor,' yes. They can't qualify for free legal aid because they make just a little too much money—but certainly not enough to pay the fees of the average attorney."

"How do you survive?"

"Me, personally, do you mean? Oh, I have a regular practice, too—ordinary stuff. As for keeping the clinic up and running, it isn't easy, but we do manage. We have volunteer lawyers who help out now and then. And you'd be surprised at what paralegals can do, with proper training and supervision, in teaching people to handle their own cases. It'd be great if you could find time to talk to my staff, you know. I could arrange a little in-service seminar, perhaps..."

Alex smiled. "Do you handle a lot of trusts and big estates around here, Fiona?"

"Everybody needs a will," Fiona said comfortably, "don't you agree? And the clinic makes ends meet because we do charge fees, of course. I don't think people truly appreciate something that's completely free. Still, we handle a simple divorce for a tenth of what other lawyers charge, and we see lots of child-custody cases and complaints about landlords." She stood. "But I'm keeping you from concentrating. If you want a copy of that file to take with you, just ask Amy at the front desk."

Alex smiled and shook her head. "I'll read it here. It's huge, and I wouldn't want to use up your photocopy budget."

Fiona grinned and left the room. Alex propped her elbow on the edge of the desk and rested her forehead against her fingertips, shading her eyes from the glare of the lamp while she read the will again.

It was difficult to concentrate on the convoluted language, and her eyes stung. But she wasn't tired; she couldn't be, for last night she'd slept like a baby.

She was just restless, that was the problem, Alex thought. She'd spent too many hours today sitting still and reading papers. If only she could get a little fresh air, maybe walk a while...

Or go beachcombing, perhaps? she asked herself wryly. She shook her head and turned back to the document.

That was when the answer jumped out at her. She blinked and looked at it again. Yes, that clause said precisely what she thought it said—no more, no less.

She thought it through, plotting a plan of attack, and then went looking for Fiona. The door directly across the narrow hallway from Alex's borrowed cubicle was open now. The lights were on, but the room was empty, and as Alex turned toward the receptionist's desk, she overheard a last-minute bit of advice from the waiting room in a voice as warm as velvet—a voice she could not mistake.

"Tell the landlord what your demands are, just the way you told me a few minutes ago when we practiced it," Kane was saying, "and let me know how it turns out." He shook the client's hand and turned back toward the offices, directly into Alex's path.

She looked him over from head to toe. She was frankly surprised; he was actually wearing a pin-striped shirt and polished shoes. No tie, of course, and no jacket—but no jeans, either. His trousers had a sharp crease, and the way they fit emphasized his narrow hips and made him look about eight feet tall.

"Do you know," she said sweetly, "I'm a little worried about you, Kane. This is the first time I've ever seen you look startled about anything. Is that the lake effect, too?"

A muscle twitched at the corner of his mouth. "I didn't expect Fiona would be able to talk you into volunteering for her favorite charity, that's for sure."

Alex plowed on. "Three weeks of not practicing law and you're already losing your touch at keeping a straight face... Oh, I beg your pardon. You're still dishing out legal advice, aren't you? It's just not the conventional sort."

Kane shrugged. "It happens to be a straightforward landlord-tenant dispute. If I started writing letters about it, the next thing you know everybody would be in court. If she just goes and talks to the man as one human being to another—"

Fiona appeared from the back of the building. "Well, I see you two are both free," she said brightly.

"In more ways than one," Alex muttered. "Do you spend a lot of time here, Kane?"

"I help out once in a while. Why?"

Fiona put one hand on Alex's shoulder and the other on Kane's arm. "Look, it's getting late. Everything else will wait till tomorrow. Why don't you two knock off and take in a movie or something?"

"Good idea," Alex said, "except for the movie part." She handed Fiona the folder she held and went to get her briefcase.

Kane was leaning against her car when she came out of the clinic. His windbreaker was zipped halfway up and his hair was ruffling in the breeze. "You look angry," he said.

"Congratulations!" She reached around him to unlock the door.

"Why?"

"You told me you were burned-out."

"I am."

"You said you were tired of practicing law."

"I think I did put it that way, yes, but—"

"Then why are you here at the clinic volunteering?"

Kane sighed. "I'm not just volunteering, Alex. I'm going to practice with Fiona."

Alex threw her briefcase into the car as hard as she could. "That is the most ridiculous thing I've ever heard!"

"You have such a warm way of putting things," Kane said. "It opens up lines of communication and makes one long to confide in you."

Alex was furious. "Do you honestly expect me to be understanding? Are you crazy? You've been telling me for days you don't want to practice law anymore, Kane!"

"I didn't write the whole profession off, Alex. I—"

"You said all the joy had gone out of it. You can't possibly deny that."

He nodded. "That's quite true. There's not much joy in the way Pence Whitfield operates. Fourteen-hour days, hundred-hour weeks. How many of the partners do you suppose attended their kids' birthday parties last year?"

"Stop trying to change the subject!" Alex said angrily. "So you're going to substitute this, instead. Volunteering your time to deal with petty landlord problems."

"Not all the problems are petty, and I'm not exactly volunteering. Fiona's made me a generous offer."

"Generous by whose standards? I'll bet you won't even be making a decent living!"

His hands came to rest on her upper arms, and the strength of his grip sent a surge of heat through her body. "Alex," he said grimly, "can't you understand that I'm not as worried about making a living as I am about having a life?"

She stared up at him, eyes wide. When he let her go, she sagged against the side of the car and absently began rubbing the hot spots on her arms where his hands had rested.

"Sorry," he muttered. "I didn't mean to hurt you." He started to walk away.

"Kane!" Alex called. "Wait!"

He stopped, but didn't turn.

Alex took a deep breath. "I'm angry, yes," she managed. "But more than that, I'm hurt. Why didn't you tell me what you were planning?"

His voice was quiet, almost flat. "Because I figured you'd react exactly like this."

What could she say to that? He'd known exactly how she'd feel about it and no doubt hadn't wanted to face her reaction. "So you just kept leading me on," she said bitterly.

After a long silent moment, he went back to her. "Let's walk."

She fell into step beside him, her shoulders hunched and her arms folded across her chest in a classic self-protective pose. "Why, Kane? Tell me why you're doing this."

He sighed. "Because no amount of money can buy time."

Time, she thought. This wasn't the first occasion he'd brought it up. He seemed obsessed with the idea of time....

Alex's breath caught in her throat. "Are you—" Her voice came out as little more than a squeak. She tried again. "Kane, you're not terminally ill or something?"

Please, she thought, as if begging some amorphous all-powerful being. *Not that. Never that! Don't let the world be without him....*

"I don't have cancer, no. But aren't we all terminally ill in a way? We're not promised an infinite number of tomorrows."

Alex didn't know whether to be relieved at the reassurance or annoyed at his reasoning. "Oh, please," she groaned. "Let's not have the philosophical lecture again about how nobody gets out of this world alive. It's trite and pointless and stupid."

He shot her a look. "I liked you a lot better when you thought I was dying," he complained.

Alex thought it prudent to ignore that.

"All right, I won't lecture you," Kane said. "The point is that I want to make the most of what I have. I want to have time for important things, for family and friends. How many friends do you have, Alex? I don't mean acquaintances, but honest, true, close friends?"

"Half a dozen, I suppose," she said stiffly.

"And when was the last time you spent any time with them? Any one of them?"

She'd seen them all just last week, she almost said, at Joanna Adler's baby shower. Everyone had managed to make time for that . . .

. . . *and I was there for no more than fifteen minutes. Just long enough to share my greetings and farewells.*

"Aunt Tess was my best friend," Kane said quietly. "But it wasn't till the week before she died that she ever told me she loved me. She would have told me before, I think, but I wasn't around."

"You couldn't help that, Kane."

"The hospice volunteers that she'd trained and coordinated all those years were taking care of her. She was surrounded by friends."

Alex privately thought that Kane's aunt Tess would have been more likely to be barking orders than uttering soft and sentimental phrases. Still, even if it wasn't the standard deathbed scene, it was a comforting picture. "That's beautiful," she said.

"Yes, isn't it? But do you know what I started thinking? If I were to find myself in that situation, there is no one who'd be there for me."

"Kane, what are you, thirty-two, thirty-three? Don't you think you're being awfully morbid?"

"Perhaps, a little—but it's true. My parents are dead, and my sisters are absorbed in their own lives. I have hundreds of acquaintances, but very few friends. No one, in fact, that I could confidently call on if I was in trouble." He added softly, "No one who wouldn't mind, even if I was a bloody nuisance."

"Kane, that's—"

"I'm not feeling sorry for myself," he said hastily. "I'm stating the facts. You can't have friends unless you *are* a friend. And you can't be much of a friend when you're always so far from home that even your secretary isn't sure where you are."

She bristled a little. "If that's a nasty crack about me because Sharon couldn't find me when Joanna's baby was born..."

"It wasn't. As a matter of fact, I'd forgotten all about that. I was thinking about myself. I don't want the rest of my life to be the same way, Alex. I want to have people around me who really know me, and who like me despite my shortcomings, not just because of what I can do for them."

Alex shook her head. "And you think throwing away everything you've worked for is the answer?"

Kane didn't seem to hear. "When the time comes, I want my wife to be my best friend, not some kind of housekeeper and nanny I see once a week when I come home for fresh clothes. And I want to have time for my kids. I want to take them fishing, and teach them to swim, and be bored by every piano recital and school play they're ever in."

Alex sighed. "You talk about time, but this new job of yours isn't exactly going to be a cream puff. You'll have to work much longer hours to make the same kind of money you did at Pence Whitfield."

"Oh, I'm quite aware that can't be done," he said cheerfully. "There simply aren't enough hours in the year to make up the difference between Pence Whitfield's rates and Fiona's."

"All right, so maybe you don't mind lowering your standard of living. But it's going to take a lot of twenty-dollar retainer fees just to buy the basic groceries, Kane, and you're going to have to work harder to get those fees. You can't specialize in a town this size, so there'll be more study time to keep up with everything you have to know. And those little problems that look so interesting right now because they're new and different will be petty and frustrating when you face the same sort of thing every day."

He stopped walking and looked down at her again. His brow was furrowed, and his hands were thrust hard in the pockets of the windbreaker.

He didn't like what he was hearing, Alex thought. But that didn't matter, because he had to hear it, anyway.

She went on almost sadly, "Think about it, Kane. The more time you spend with Fiona's fascinating clients, the less you'll have for your friends. The more charity cases you take on, the tougher it will be to earn the income to support that wife and kids you say you want. It's a no-win situation. And you won't have the respect of your peers anymore, either. People in the Twin Cities already think you were fired. If you don't come back, they'll be certain of it."

There was a long silence. "Who cares?" he said.

He sounded tired, as if every ounce of energy had drained out of his body.

Alex felt a flood of sympathy for him and had to force herself not to show it. Sympathy wasn't what he needed right now; what he had to hear was ruthless honesty. If she could just make him admit that his perfect pastoral picture might quickly sour, she could capitalize on this opening.

But before she could find the words, he said, "Let them think what they like. All of them." And he turned on his heel and walked away.

THE ARGUMENT HAD LEFT Alex emotionally exhausted. It took considerable effort to retrace her steps, partly because she'd been so absorbed that she had paid no attention to the direction they'd walked, or how far they'd come. By the time she found her way back to her car, she had started to picture herself as a permanent fixture in downtown Duluth, wandering alone and in exile forever.

Kane was nowhere to be seen, and the storefront was dark. Alex shivered a little and drove quickly back to the Guest House.

There was a message waiting for her from Neville Morgan. She glanced at the clock and, crumpling the message, dropped it into the pocket of her linen skirt. It had been hours since he called; she'd catch him at the office in the morning.

She sank onto the couch in her sitting room, longing for a bath but too weary even to run a tub of water. She was also too weary to care what she ate. She picked up an apple from the fruit basket on the side table and gnawed on it absentmindedly.

Another attempt, she thought, and another failure. For a few minutes there, she'd really thought she'd been getting through to Kane.

And perhaps she had, she reflected. Maybe that was why he'd walked away—because he knew she was right, and he just couldn't quite bring himself to admit it yet.

Perhaps he'd simply wanted to be on his own so he could think about it quietly, and the next time she saw him . . .

"Don't bet the rent on it," she muttered.

She finished the apple and tossed the core into the crystal coaster on the coffee table. Beside the coaster lay the unfinished pink-and-blue quilt, her needle already inserted for the next stitch. She picked it up.

The soft fabric against her fingertips, the flash of the needle, the easy rhythm of the stitches, were soothing as always, and time inched by as she worked.

Just this tiny section, she thought, and I'll go and have a bath. One more bit and I'll call down for dinner. Then I'll call Joanna.

But she didn't stop until her hand cramped from the unaccustomed position. Setting the quilting hoop down, she laughed a little at her lack of discipline and reached for the telephone.

Joanna was home, her husband said, but she was feeding the baby, and he didn't know if she could come to the phone.

In the background, Alex heard Joanna's voice murmuring a question, and a moment later she came on the line. "Alex! What a treat to talk to you again!"

The tone of her voice warmed Alex's heart. Kane had implied this afternoon that neither of them had real friends, but he had been wrong about her, at least.

"I hope it's not a bad time to call."

"Oh, no. It's just a trick to hold the telephone and the baby at the same time. Are you home?"

"No, not yet. And I may not be for a while."

"The estate must be complicated."

"Yes . . . and so are other things." Alex hesitated. Joanna might have some insight that would help her deal with Kane, she thought. After all, her friend's profession was dealing with people, matching them to the right jobs, keeping them happy. "I'm running into snags all over the place." She hesitated. Joanna would keep the information confidential, she was sure. Still, it was an inside problem. Perhaps she shouldn't bring Joanna into it at all.

"There are always plenty of those, aren't there?" Joanna said cheerfully. "Sometimes I'm glad I've got a few weeks of no troubles but baby ones... Sorry, did you say something? The telephone slipped."

Alex said slowly, "It was nothing. I'll sort it all out."

"Of course you will. Wait till you see this baby, Alex. He's the most precious..."

What was it Kane had said this afternoon? *No one who wouldn't mind, even if I was a bloody nuisance*—yes, that was it.

Joanna has her hands full, Alex told herself. And her mind was very much on that brand-new baby, which was precisely where it ought to be. Still...

You can't have friends unless you are a friend. She could almost hear Kane's words echoing through her head.

"Of course I'm a friend," she said.

There was a momentary silence, then Joanna said, "You certainly are. Will you be home for the baby's christening in a couple of weeks, do you suppose?"

A tap sounded from the hallway. Alex dragged the telephone across the room and opened the door to let in Mrs. Keith. "There's another call for you, Miss Jacobi, from a Mr. Morgan. I'm sorry, but he was quite insistent that I interrupt you."

Alex nodded. "Joanna? Sorry, I've got to go. I'll call you later about the christening."

Mrs. Keith had been quite accurate; Neville Morgan was not only insistent but impatient. "I talked to Paul Wintergreen this evening," he said. "I expected perhaps you'd be with him, since you weren't at the hotel earlier."

"You did give me two assignments when you sent me up here," she reminded him.

"So you were with Kane? That's really what I'm calling about. I was expecting a report today—something a little more detailed than what you gave me on the telephone yesterday. You know I can't do a thing until you let me know how the negotiations are proceeding."

Alex chewed her lip. She couldn't lie to Neville Morgan; airily promising success would only lead to trouble down the road if she couldn't ultimately produce a meek and chastened Kane like a rabbit from a hat. But she could hardly tell the truth, either.

Neville, old buddy, she thought, *if you think the shack on the shore was bad, just wait'll you hear about his new partner and his new practice.*

But that approach wouldn't earn her any points at Pence Whitfield. Besides, she wasn't ready to throw in the towel just yet, was she?

She compromised on the strictest kind of truth. "He hasn't exactly told me what it would take for him to come back, Mr. Morgan."

"Nonsense. You just have to be firm and let him know that you've got the authority to deal. And then you offer him the damned moon on a silver platter, Alex. Anything he wants."

For a moment she wasn't sure she'd heard him correctly. "Anything?" Her voice was a little shaky.

"Anything. Go ahead, tell him that. Hell, if he wants to marry my daughter, I'll lock her in her room on bread and water till she agrees. But get him, Alex." He hung up with a firm click.

She sat there for a couple of minutes with the telephone dangling in her hand. *Anything he wants...*

What had Kane said he wanted this afternoon? *Time.* No amount of money could buy the time that was necessary to develop friends and to nurture a marriage and a family.

But that was the only point he'd made, she realized. All Kane really wanted was a less-hectic schedule, fewer business trips and more days off. Not all that much. And if the alternative was losing him altogether... Pence Whitfield would jump at the compromise.

Why had she been so dense for so long?

Mostly because Kane had protested loudly about being tired of law, Alex thought. But in fact, that wasn't what he had been saying at all. He didn't want to get away from the profession. He loved it as much as she did. And if he could practice at Pence Whitfield under his own conditions...

He could have it all, Alex thought. Everything he wanted.

She replaced the receiver and stretched, then laughed lightheartedly. "We've won," she whispered. "Kane by holding out, and me by accidentally cooperating with him. We've won!"

She didn't even particularly mind anymore that he'd manipulated her into helping him get to this point. It was worth it, to have everything work out in the end.

Now all she had to do was find Kane and tell him the good news.

CHAPTER EIGHT

KANE WAS NOWHERE to be found. When he'd left Alex at her car, he seemed to have disappeared into thin air. He didn't answer his telephone, and on Tuesday evening when she drove out to Inglenook, there wasn't a light to be seen, and the Ferrari was gone.

Those things didn't bother her particularly. He could be anywhere—grocery shopping, walking on that sandy beach they'd been to the other day, or just driving along the shore to clear his head and think. But when she tried the back door, intending to leave a note on the kitchen table, she was startled to find it locked.

She almost panicked at that and had to talk to herself very severely before she calmed down again. Kane hadn't said that he *never* locked the doors, she reminded herself. The fact that he hadn't closed the place up when she was around didn't mean that he left it standing open no matter where he went.

She left her card in the mailbox where he would certainly find it whenever he came home. There wasn't even a scrap of junk mail in the box, so he hadn't been gone long, Alex concluded. Or else the next-door neighbor was picking up the mail for him....

But why she should rush to assume that he had left town was beyond her. He was probably finding the isolation of the cabin getting to him, that was all.

Alex stopped by the storefront clinic on Wednesday and asked to see Fiona.

"She's stacked up with appointments," the receptionist said. "The volunteer who was to come in this morning canceled, so Fiona's the only attorney here. But I'm sure she'll find a few minutes between clients for you."

"That's fine. May I see the file again that I was working on last time?" As the receptionist went to get it, Alex added easily, "It must be difficult for Fiona to handle all this by herself."

"It can be a handful, that's for sure."

"I guess she's pretty happy to have Kane's help."

The receptionist thumbed through the drawer and tugged the file out. "She will be, if they ever get the details worked out. He hasn't settled into a regular schedule yet." Then she shot a worried glance at Alex, perhaps afraid she shouldn't have said anything of the sort.

Alex wasn't surprised. Of course he hadn't settled into a schedule yet, and of course the details hadn't been worked out. It was one more bit of confirmation for her that Kane didn't want to commit himself here as long as there was a chance to get what he wanted at Pence Whitfield. No doubt Fiona knew it, too.

A few minutes later the receptionist directed her to Fiona's office at the very back of the building. It was no larger than the other cubicles, but one wall held a scattering of family photographs, and a brass stand in the corner boasted a truly beautiful assortment of green plants.

"They look so healthy," Alex said. "Of course, for all I know you could be raising poison ivy there."

Fiona laughed. "Not a bad idea. I could send cuttings to people who volunteer and then don't show up to work.

I gather you've found something helpful?'' She gestured at the folder Alex was carrying.

"How would your client like to run a used-car lot?"

Fiona frowned. "I think it's probably the last thing on her mind. Why?"

"Look." Alex flipped open the will and put it on Fiona's desk. "Right there in section eight, clause seventeen. Among the things the trustee is to provide for the child's welfare is a reliable means of transport."

"Yes. That's not uncommon."

"But this one says he must provide a car. And it doesn't say anything about how often he must do so, or what happens to the existing car. In fact, your client could pick up her new vehicle from the dealer, drive it down the street to the first used-car lot, pocket the cash, then call up the trustee for another one." She sat back in her chair with a flourish. "Unless she'd rather start up her own business, of course. And it's not just cars. The way that will is written, she could wholesale everything from disposable diapers to bicycles to school uniforms."

Fiona pulled a pair of reading glasses out of her desk drawer and perched them on the end of her nose. "I'd missed that entirely." She looked at Alex over the rim of the lenses and said, "It does say 'shall' instead of 'may,' doesn't it? Of course, it wouldn't be ethical. . . ."

Alex saw a twinkle in Fiona's eyes. "Of course it's not ethical. In fact, I wouldn't seriously suggest that she do it. But I suspect the trustee isn't a fool, and if you were to hint that the proceeds might go to investigating his use of the remaining money, he might decide to be reasonable."

Fiona reached for a pen. "It's worth a try."

"Let me know how it turns out." Alex slid to the edge of her chair. "By the way, do you know where Kane is? I've been trying to reach him."

Fiona didn't look up from her legal pad. "He went down to Minneapolis for a couple of days."

"Subletting his apartment, no doubt," Alex said, and watched for a reaction.

"He didn't say," Fiona said absently. She was still absorbed in the will.

Alex wasn't surprised. But the lack of reaction convinced her that Fiona, too, wasn't so sure the details would ever be worked out.

Alex just hoped that whatever Kane was up to, he wasn't planning to stop by Pence Whitfield for a chat with Neville Morgan. If he talked to the partners right now, he could inadvertently cut himself out of the best deal he'd ever be likely to make in his life.

AFTER A FULL WEEK in the warehouse, Alex had become so accustomed to the monotonous files of papers that she was concerned she might miss something important in the smudgy carbon sheets. Most of Geoffrey's correspondence was not like his exchange with the landscape architect. In fact, most of it was downright dull, and she had to force herself to concentrate on each word, instead of letting her mind skate off onto much more interesting subjects.

She was so busy thinking about Kane's trip while she was reading a long letter from Geoffrey to an old school chum that she almost missed the reference to Ralph. Geoffrey was complaining about his nephew's habits and the way he lived. "But of course when I'm dead it will be a different story," he went on cryptically. "He'll have to keep up appearances then." She read on eagerly, but the letter segued into another subject entirely.

Alex held the page up with a frown and read it again. Hadn't Kane told her that Ralph lived in a bad section of town? And though she was no expert on Duluth neighborhoods, the address Ralph had given her certainly didn't sound ritzy.

So if Geoffrey wasn't complaining about Ralph's living beyond his means, what was he referring to? Did he mean that after his uncle was dead, Ralph would have to scramble to put on a show of affluence to keep his creditors at bay—or did he mean that he would have plenty of funds and a new status in the community to uphold?

"It doesn't matter," Alex muttered. "If I've got reasonable doubt about what he meant, then any competent attorney could convince a court to look into it."

And that meant Ralph Wintergreen could well have a case, after all.

Alex looked through another couple of folders while she thought it over. Nothing in the surrounding letters seemed questionable, or even open to interpretation. Of course, she reminded herself, Geoffrey's intricate filing system didn't allow her to easily pull out his other letters to the same old school chum for comparison. She would have to stumble across them individually as she worked her way through the boxes, and that might take weeks.

Should she immediately tell Paul what she'd found? Call Neville Morgan for advice first? Keep the knowledge of the letter to herself for the moment and wait to see if anything else turned up before she decided what to do?

The last choice was the riskiest, she reminded herself. This might be a critical development, and there was no excuse to postpone telling Paul. Besides, attorneys had a moral obligation to keep their clients informed in a timely manner of what was going on in their cases. She would work a little longer and think out her new strategy, then go back to the Guest House and clean up before she took the letter to Paul's office. She could hardly show up there in jeans and a sweatshirt. And perhaps she should call Neville Morgan first. . . .

Before she'd made up her mind on how best to proceed, Paul came around the corner of her makeshift office. Alex thought he looked a little surprised at her garb, but he didn't comment.

"Hello," he said cheerfully. "How's the prospector? I thought perhaps you needed a break and some real coffee, and since you're keeping yourself shut up here all the time, I brought it down."

Alex pushed the carton away. There was no point trying to work if he was going to stay. It wasn't much comfort for her to reflect that even if Paul was wasting her time, at least he was paying for it.

Paul handed her a mug. "It looks like slow progress."

Alex looked around at the twin walls of boxes. On one side of her table was a neat long row of unopened cartons, just as the office boy had stacked them last week before she started to work. On the other side of the table was a second, much smaller pile of cartons she had completed. It was messier, and the unsealed boxes weren't stacked as high.

"I still think a secretary or two would be a good idea."

Alex sipped her coffee and set the mug down. "A secretary would probably have missed—" She stopped abruptly, and then gave a mental shrug. What did it matter if she hadn't talked to Neville Morgan yet? She'd already decided to tell Paul about the letter right away, hadn't she? "—what I found this afternoon."

She picked up the single sheet of onionskin, the carbon of Geoffrey's letter, and handed it to him.

He read it, and frowned. "I don't quite see what you mean."

Alex explained the dual interpretations. "And there might be some other possible meanings I haven't even considered yet," she finished.

Paul shrugged. "I can't see that it makes a difference, though. The will is so clear, and this is so vague. . . ."

"What's important is that this leaves room for a legitimate difference of opinion about your uncle's intentions toward Ralph. That's certainly enough for Ralph to make a case. He might even win."

"Based on this?" Paul flicked at the onionskin with a contemptuous finger. "A single phrase in an obscure old letter addressed to somebody Ralph's probably never even met? How could Ralph even know about this?"

"That's beside the point, Paul. You can't prove he doesn't know about it."

"Look, I've never heard of the old codger Geoffrey was writing to. How could Ralph have found him?"

"All I've uncovered is an indication, I admit. The reference isn't clear. But—"

"That's the most sensible thing I've heard you say."

Alex ignored the growl. "But based on this letter or something like it, a good attorney could demand access to Geoffrey's files."

She saw Paul's quick glance around the room.

"All of them," Alex added. "He can do the same search I'm doing."

"And find the same thing you have—nothing."

"Do you want to gamble on that, Paul? True, I've found only one doubtful paragraph so far, but there may well be others. With enough of them, Ralph can build a case."

He paced the warehouse floor, head down. When he came back to the pool of light that surrounded her table, he pointed out, "Ralph said he had evidence. The way he described it made it sound as if he had a single document or statement, not a collage of bits and pieces like you're talking about."

"Perhaps he does, Paul. He may not even know about this particular letter."

"You've talked to Geoffrey's employees?"

"Not all of them. The ones I've reached don't seem to know anything. I don't know what Ralph has, Paul. But I'm convinced now that he has something."

"And you're suddenly siding with Ralph."

"I would never let a personal reaction to a client, no matter what it was, affect my judgment about his case," Alex said sharply. "I'm not siding with anyone. I'm giving you the facts as I see them."

"So what are you suggesting?"

Alex bit her lip and took a long breath. "I think you should consider a settlement."

Paul's voice wasn't intimate and low and breathy any longer. It was almost shrill with disbelief. "Just call Ralph up and tell him I'll give him money that Geoffrey clearly wanted me to have?"

"That's not exactly what I mean. Offering a deal now would probably only create trouble. It could lead Ralph to believe we've found something damning—something that might give him the whole estate—and then he'd be unlikely to settle for a portion. But if and when he does make a move to file suit . . . then, instead of fighting, I think we should negotiate a deal."

"Over this." Paul picked up the onionskin again.

Alex was afraid he was going to tear it to shreds. She took it out of his hand and stowed it safely in her briefcase.

"It's not right," Paul muttered. "He can't win on this kind of thing."

"We don't know what sort of evidence he's got," Alex reminded him.

"I still say he's bluffing."

"He might be, Paul." She paused, then went on softly, "But even if he is and he's eventually thrown out of court, the case could drag on for years. You said yourself you thought that might be part of the strategy—just keeping things in an uproar as long as possible."

He nodded reluctantly.

"It's going to cost you more to fight than it will to reach an agreement. Paul, just the expense of preparing for the possibility of a fight is going to be stiff. In the last week I've run up your legal bill by more than fifteen thousand dollars, and I'm not a quarter of the way through the paperwork."

"So you won't fight it?"

After a moment Alex replied, "It's a judgment call. Under these circumstances, if my opinion and the client's conflict, I'll do what my client wants. Yes, I'll fight it if you insist, and I won't do it halfheartedly, either. But I happen to believe there are times when the best way to win a lawsuit is not to fight it at all."

The words seemed to echo in her head. Kane had said something like that, hadn't he, about the Quadrangle deal? *Sometimes the best deal is no deal . . .*

"Sometimes it's better in the long run," Alex went on gently, "to swallow your pride and have the whole thing over with—and at least know what the final bill is going to be."

Paul shook his head.

Alex thought that the gesture didn't indicate disagreement as much as dissatisfaction with the system. "If Ralph's attorney does win the right to go through these papers," she said, "you'll need someone like me sitting here every minute watching him, so he doesn't slip something in that doesn't belong."

"At five hundred dollars an hour."

"It won't be cheap, no."

"What you're really saying is that any joker can tie things up for years and end up getting something he's not entitled to."

"No. What I'm saying is that you're going to spend the money one way or the other. Why not get it over with, Paul, so you don't have to fret all the time about what Ralph may do next?"

"Neville Morgan wouldn't like to hear you talking about swallowing pride and sacrificing principles."

"Neville Morgan didn't get where he is by being idealistic," Alex said curtly. "I've given you the best legal advice I can at this moment. And I'll tell Mr. Morgan that, too."

There was a long thoughtful silence. Then Paul said in a completely different tone, "All right. I believe that you've thought it all through, and that you have my best interests at heart. How much do you think Ralph would settle for?"

PAUL SUGGESTED DINNER, of course, so they could continue their business discussion. Alex refused. There was little more to talk about now; the next move was Ralph's, and all they could do in the meantime was wait.

Besides, she was feeling particularly restless, in no mood for sitting still in some elaborate restaurant and chatting with Paul, no matter what the subject. So she said a firm good-night to him at the warehouse.

Gentleman that he was, Paul waited till she'd started her car and then followed her almost back to the Guest House. But the moment Alex realized he had gone on about his own business, she pulled off to the side of the street and simply sat there for a while.

She did not want to go back to her room for another quiet meal, another evening alone. She especially did not want to be faced at this moment with the need to write another progress report on the Wintergreen estate.

It wasn't that she thought Neville Morgan would disagree with her conclusions exactly, but she knew it would take her best efforts to persuade him. It would be far better to let the progress report wait till morning, when she was fresh.

She put the car into gear again and took the scenic highway out toward Inglenook. She could at least see if Kane was home yet.

In the past couple of days Alex had gotten into the habit of driving past Inglenook no matter where she was actually headed or how far it was out of her way. If she did that, she'd reasoned the first time she made the detour, she was bound to see the Ferrari within a reasonable time of its reappearance. And if she needed an excuse to stop by, well, she'd figure that out when the need arose. It wouldn't take much of an excuse, anyway; there was plenty she wanted to talk to Kane about. And once she mentioned Neville Morgan's name and the new liberal terms he had made for Kane's return, she was sure Kane would want to talk to her, as well.

She wondered what he was doing in Minneapolis. Getting the car serviced? Catching up on the personal business of the past few weeks? Dating Neville Morgan's daughter?

Now why had Lisle Morgan come to mind? she wondered. Then she remembered the remark Neville had made the last time she had talked to him. *If Kane wants to marry my daughter, I'll lock her in her room on bread and water till she agrees.*

Alex laughed at herself for letting the comment stick in her memory. It had been a purely rhetorical statement, that was all, made to emphasize the partners' willingness to make a deal on any terms. It was silly to think of Lisle Morgan and Kane as a couple. The only time Alex had ever seen them together was at that Christmas party....

She frowned. They had certainly seemed to gravitate toward each other that night; only minutes after Kane's chat with Alex about the Reynolds case in that secluded little nook, he'd been dancing with Lisle Morgan. Had she been waiting for him?

And who cared if she was? Alex asked herself.

It was a throwaway question, a careless query that had no answer. That was why the reply that sprang to life inside her came as a complete shock.

"I care," she said aloud.

She tried to laugh at her foolishness. It had only been a party, and a year and a half ago at that. What kind of idiotic woman would be jealous over it now?

A woman who'd been thrown into an unusually intimate situation with a man she admired, Alex realized. A woman who'd overreacted to that intimate situation. A woman trembling on the verge of a romantic entanglement....

"Oh, for heaven's sake," she chastised herself. "This is ridiculous."

Yes, she admired Kane Forrestal—his talent, his quick mind, his resourcefulness, his accomplishments, his gift for the law. Yes, she liked him—his sense of humor, that rich lazy voice, the way his eyes lit when he smiled, the effect his kisses had on her.

But to have to admit that she was as infatuated with him as an adolescent schoolgirl with a crush on a rock star, that was too much.

A horn blared behind her and a car emblazoned with the name of a pizza-delivery service swept by. The driver's state of mind was obvious from the way he glared at Alex.

She muttered an apology under her breath. She'd been so preoccupied she hadn't realized she'd let her car slow to a crawl. Every driver on the highway was probably annoyed with her.

She tried to talk sense into herself, convince herself she wasn't hopelessly naive. Kane had paid a flattering amount of attention to her in the past week, it was true, and she had enjoyed it. But that didn't mean she had to take it seriously. After all, the man had hardly remembered who she was at first, when she'd called him the day she'd arrived in Duluth....

"And you were annoyed about it, too," she accused herself. "You were furious, down deep, that he could have overlooked you, forgotten you like that."

She was so absorbed in her own reflections that she drove straight by Inglenook, not even registering that there was a vehicle in the drive until she was past. And when it did register, she craned her neck to try to get a glimpse of it in the rearview mirror. It hadn't been the Ferrari, she was sure of that, but an older bigger car, instead.

Probably someone simply turning around, she thought.

It was half a mile before she herself found a place to pull off the road and turn around, and by the time she got back to Inglenook the car she'd seen was gone. But the Ferrari was in the drive, and there were lights in the house. It looked, in fact, as if every lamp in the whole place was on.

Kane's home, she thought. *He's finally home.*

Alex felt an overwhelming sense of pressure in her chest, a potent combination of excitement and fear. It was almost exactly the same sensation she'd had the first time she took her place in a real courtroom and argued a real case.

And what was causing that internal uproar this time? It was an uncomfortable question, and Alex was not certain she wanted to look too hard for the answer. Not just now, at any rate.

The main door was open, and only a screen stood in Alex's way. She paused when she caught a glimpse of him inside the kitchen. He looked different, she thought. A little tired, perhaps. Maybe a little older. His striped sports shirt was wrinkled and his jeans creased.

It's your imagination, she told herself. *It's a long drive, that's all.*

Her soft-soled shoes had made no sound on the deck, but just as she raised her hand to knock, Kane turned toward the door as if he'd sensed her presence. Alex's gaze met his, and the pressure in her chest grew a little, as if a giant hand was tightening its clutch.

It was time to stop kidding herself, she thought. It was all nice and sweet to say she admired Kane, that she'd like to have him as a mentor and a friend. That was true, yes.

But it certainly wasn't the whole truth. She wanted a lot more than that.

She swallowed hard and groped for some flippant comment that would break the ice left by the way they had parted on that downtown street. Instead, she was shocked to hear herself saying huskily, "I missed you, Kane."

That has got to be the stupidest thing you've ever said, she upbraided herself. *Why don't you just finish it off, Jacobi? Why don't you tell him you love him, too? You might as well, because it's true....*

The admission was not as much of a shock as she would have expected it to be, and she realized that the knowledge must have been hovering just under the surface of her mind for some time.

When had it happened? she asked herself. When she had found herself thinking of him as an anchor in a crazy world, an anchor she would very much like to hold on to? Or had it been even before that—as far back as that first night at the Guest House? Had she put on that flattering little dress to counteract his comments, or because she wanted to look her loveliest for him? And had she enjoyed their conversation because she loved the idea of negotiating, or because she had simply taken delight in his presence and his attention?

Kane asked, "Are you going to come in or just stand out there with the mosquitoes?" And then, as she stepped into the kitchen, he added very softly, "I missed you, too."

The pressure in Alex's chest decreased a notch, making it slightly easier to breathe.

If he missed me, she thought, *maybe he cares about me a little. Maybe, if I'm lucky, more than a little.*

He'd said he wanted to settle down, build a family. He'd said he wanted his wife to be his best friend. Lisle Morgan certainly didn't fit that mold.

But maybe I do, Alex thought. *Maybe I do....*

It was the most natural thing in the world to walk across the room and straight into his arms. She was secure there, and safe, and at peace—at least she was until he kissed her, and then tiny packets of dynamite began to explode in series along her veins. She closed her eyes and cupped her hands about his face, uttering a soft little moan.

"It's nice to be missed," Kane said. His voice was low, and it tickled against her ear.

But the sensitive tips of her fingers, resting against his temples, warned her that he was smiling. She could feel the crinkle of laugh lines at the corners of his eyes. She pulled back a little, blinked and said, "I'm sorry to be a nuisance."

He laughed. "You're hardly that." His hands slid slowly from her shoulders down her spine and came to rest on her waist as he gave her one last, hard quick kiss. Then he let her go. "How about having a slice of pizza and telling me what brought on that warm welcome?"

He turned away to pick up the pizza box from the kitchen table. Alex was relieved; at least she had a chance to fight down the flood of embarrassed color without him watching.

What an insane thing to do, she thought, to throw herself into his arms like that. And now he wanted an explanation. Well, she couldn't blame him.

"So that's what the car was," she said thoughtfully.

Kane looked at her with one eyebrow raised.

"The pizza delivery. I came by a few minutes ago, and in the dark I missed the driveway. I didn't expect to see a car there, I guess."

"Lost again, Alex?"

She couldn't quite decide whether to be relieved because she'd succeeded in changing the subject or annoyed at the teasing, but she concluded that bristling would be her best defense. "I haven't been lost in three days, Kane. I'm actually learning my way around. It's not such a bad little town, after all."

"Of course not. It really isn't the town itself that has a way of grabbing you, though. It's—"

"Don't tell me. The lake effect."

He rewarded her with a smile. "Of course." He piled plates, napkins and soda cans atop the pizza box and led the way through the living room and out to a screened porch that faced the lake. She could hear a whispery, rhythmic sloshing from the shore as the waves exhausted themselves against the rocks.

"It's too warm inside," he said. "The house needs to air a while after being shut up for days." He set the pizza down on a low table and indicated the porch swing, which hung from massive chains anchored in the ceiling.

The swing creaked comfortably as Alex settled herself at one end. Kane put a piece of pizza on a plate and handed it to her, then sat down beside her. "So tell me about—"

Alex interrupted. "How was your trip?"

The corner of his mouth twitched in a tiny smile. If there'd been more light on the porch, Alex was certain she'd have seen a twinkle in his eyes, too.

"Not as useful as I'd hoped."

"You didn't talk to anybody at Pence Whitfield, did you?"

Kane's eyebrows shot up. "No. I was visiting my younger sister. I stayed as far away from the office as I could."

Alex released a long relieved breath. "Good."

Kane grinned. "That was heartfelt."

She was trying to find the right words to begin telling him about the deal she'd managed to wangle for him when his free hand came to rest on the nape of her neck. His fingers were warm, and the combination of heat and massage quickly relaxed her muscles. She found herself leaning toward him. Her slice of pizza slid almost off the plate; Kane took it from her and set it aside.

Then he kissed her. He kissed her till she couldn't breathe anymore, till her body ached with wanting him and her brain was like a puddle in the sand. When he let her go, Alex wasn't sure she could sit up without support.

"I'd better quit," he said ruefully, "or I'll be having to take a dip in the lake."

"It's freezing." She was only half-conscious of what she was saying.

"Not quite. But it's close enough to have the desired effect." Kane put her plate back in her hand and said with an air of determination not to be distracted again, "Has there been any excitement around here while I've been gone? Did you find the smoking gun in Geoffrey's papers?"

Alex had forgotten all about that. "Well, sort of."

She told him about the letter and her advice to Paul.

"So you told him just to sit tight and wait," Kane summarized thoughtfully when she was done. "If Ralph doesn't have anything, there's no harm done. If he does, then Paul can settle for what it would cost him anyway if he fought."

"That's about it."

"Did you talk to Neville before you did this?"

"No. And if you mean he'd want to pursue it just because Paul has the funds to pay the fees—"

"Not quite. Neville's not Sir Lancelot, but he's not that bad." The swing creaked rhythmically. "It's not the standard solution, perhaps, but it's a lot more humane than the alternatives. I'm proud of you, Alex."

He didn't look proud, Alex thought. In fact, he was frowning a little, and she was puzzled.

"That means you're done, then," Kane went on. "No more plowing through Geoffrey's papers."

Alex smiled in relief. "No more carbon stains, no more backaches..."

The smile died away. No more excuses to stay, she thought. There would be more work on the estate later on, of course. But for now, she was free; this part of the job was complete.

She had known when Paul agreed to take her advice that she'd be going back to Minneapolis soon. But somehow it hadn't felt the same then. She certainly hadn't felt this way about it—disappointed, almost lost....

She looked up at Kane, bewildered. "I don't want to go," she whispered.

Kane's arm came around her and drew her tight against him in a convulsive grip. The pizza plate slid off her knee and clattered against the tile floor. Alex didn't hear it; she was listening only to the rhythm of her heart, which whispered that he cared for her, too, and it would be all right.

"Alex," he said hoarsely, "are you sure you know what you want?"

She remembered how she'd felt the day she'd thought he might be dangerously ill. She hadn't realized just why it had affected her so, but she had known even then that she could not bear to be without him.

She pulled him even closer. "Yes," she whispered. "I want you to stay here, not go and freeze in the lake." And then she smiled at him, a tremulous smile that promised everything. . . .

CHAPTER NINE

IF ALEX HAD GIVEN IT any thought, she would have expected the upper rooms of the house to be small and narrow and dark, tucked as they were under the slope of the roof. But the bedroom to which Kane led her was airy and pleasant and surprisingly large. Moonlight poured through the open casement windows in a big dormer that looked out over the lake. And his bed was a solid, dark wood four-poster from a long-ago era, a bed to curl up in and watch the snow fall outside.

We can do that next winter, she thought. *At Christmas, we can take time off to come up here. It's always slower in the office around the holidays. And I'm sure he'll want to keep the cabin....*

But then, as Kane kissed her again, Alex's ability to think logically vanished altogether. In any case, the only thing left to think about was him, and she would much rather abandon herself to the waves of sensual excitement that threatened to overwhelm her.

And so she deliberately let go of the power of reason and allowed herself to be swept into a raging spiral of emotion and sensation and pleasure, a storm every bit as powerful as Lake Superior at its wildest. Yet, with Kane there to hold her steady, there was no fear, no alarm, just the elation of adventure....

MUCH LATER, she smoothed a lock of hair back from his damp brow. Her fingers were shaking, and her voice was little more than a croak. "That was . . . nice."

He smiled at her, curling himself around her in a warm relaxed embrace with her head pillowed on his shoulder.

"I think . . ." she began dreamily, then paused as common sense uncomfortably intruded. Telling him that she loved him would be true enough, but was it wise? That sort of announcement called for some thinking over first.

He'd said he missed her, and he'd certainly treated her just now as if she was the most important thing in his world. But what if she was jumping to conclusions about how he felt? He might be only beginning to consider Alex as the lifelong friend he might someday marry. For her to make a sudden rash declaration of love . . .

His hand brushed softly over her hair, which was scattered wildly across his shoulder and the pillow underneath. "It will be all right," he said. "It will all work out, Alex. When two people care about each other . . ."

Alex thought for a moment that her heart was going to burst, it was so filled with love for him in that instant. Incapable of speech, she gave him a tight hug, instead, burying her face in his neck with her lips against the pulse point at the base of his throat.

He smiled down at her and very deliberately began to caress her back, each long stroke making her spine tingle and the rest of her ache with desire, and before long, everything was forgotten—everything except this new and glorious way to tell him how much he meant to her.

THE PEACEFUL RHYTHM of the waves must have been a subliminal lullaby, for when Alex awoke she was startled to see sunlight pouring through the wide-open dormer windows. Kane wasn't beside her; there was only a dented pillow and the sensual glow in every cell of her body to tell her that the night before hadn't been just a vivid dream.

It didn't bother her that he wasn't there; she knew it must be late. She stretched luxuriously and looked in vain for a clock. Finally she gave up and wrapped herself in the tartan bathrobe she found hanging on the back of the bathroom door. Barefoot, she wandered downstairs, feeling lazy and contented.

There was no evidence of him there, either, except for a fresh full pot of coffee in the kitchen. She was puzzled for a moment, because she could see the Ferrari still parked outside. In fact, he couldn't have gotten it out without moving her car, which was directly behind it. Had he taken his bike, then? But where would he have gone? And why?

Don't be silly, she chided herself. *If he'd been going to flee, he wouldn't have said what he did last night about two people caring about each other.*

Then she heard a dog bark from somewhere at the back of the house, and she stepped out onto the deck to look around.

Kane was coming up from the seawall. He was wearing cutoffs and a pullover shirt, and when he smiled at her Alex thought she'd never in her life seen a man who was so incredibly handsome. Then she realized that capering at his feet was the largest wettest dog she had ever seen. It was hard to tell just what sort of breed it was, since the long hair was drenched and dripping. Part collie, perhaps? Part Siberian husky?

"Yours?" she asked faintly.

Kane looked down at the animal just as it gleefully shook the excess water from its coat. He tried to dodge the resulting shower, with minimal success. "No, thank heaven. He belongs three houses down, but he comes up the shore to visit at low tide."

"Of course." Mixed with Alex's relief was a little annoyance with herself. He might have said he'd like a dog, but he certainly knew that the city was no place for an animal this size.

Kane held out his hand. "Look what I found."

Alex took the dark red stone and turned it over in her palm. "An agate, right?"

"It's the biggest one I've ever found on this beach. Polish it up a little and set it in a necklace." He added softly, "I was looking for something special for you—since I didn't have a red rose for your pillow this morning."

Warmth oozed through Alex's muscles.

"Shall we go back inside?" Kane said. "So I can kiss you the way I'd like, without the neighbors seeing?"

It was a wonderful kiss, long and warm and soft. Alex's knees had completely disintegrated by the time Kane released her. She sat down rather abruptly at the kitchen table.

He smiled knowingly and handed her a cup of coffee. "A little breakfast will take away that all-gone feeling." He whistled a little as he dug out a skillet.

Alex thought it unlikely that anything as mundane as food was going to change the way she felt, but she decided there was no sense in feeding his ego by telling him that. She reached for her handbag and dug out her brush. "My hair is a mess," she murmured. "It's going to take hours to get the tangles out."

"I should have warned you. That's the lake effect."

"Tangled hair?"

"No. Loss of self-control, and everything it leads to." He grinned a little and reached for a carton of eggs.

Alex spotted the clock on the kitchen wall and let out a shriek. "Is that the time?"

Kane looked at it without interest. "I suppose so. It isn't usually wrong. Why?"

"Good heavens, it's almost noon. This isn't breakfast, it's brunch. And we've got so much to talk about!"

"So talk." He whisked eggs in a measuring cup. "I can cook and listen at the same time."

"How about driving and talking at the same time? No, that won't work. We've got two cars."

"Driving where?" He tested the skillet and carefully poured in the egg mixture.

"Minneapolis, of course."

Kane tipped his head to one side quizzically. "I was just there yesterday. Why would I want to go back?"

"To take care of everything in person, right away. To talk to Neville Morgan and the partners."

"Neville and the partners," Kane mused. "Sounds like a bad rock band, doesn't it?"

"It doesn't matter what it sounds like. They're ready to give you everything you want when you go back, Kane."

He was frowning. "You surely don't still think I'm going back to Pence Whitfield."

"Of course you are. You can't be serious about staying here." But her voice wavered a little.

"Don't you ever listen? Dammit, Alex, last night you said you didn't want to go back yourself!"

"I did not! I said I didn't want to leave you. That's not the same thing at all."

He shook his head grimly. "What you said was—"

"What I meant ... Oh, what does it matter, Kane? Don't you see? You can write your own deal now. They're desperate to get you back."

"Really?"

She heard the disdain in his voice. "I swear it, Kane. Neville Morgan told me himself you can have everything you want."

"No travel?" he said crisply. "An eight-hour day? Every weekend free?"

Alex hesitated. "Maybe not quite that liberal," she began, then sat up straight. Neville Morgan had made a promise, she reminded herself. "Yes," she said firmly. "All of that."

He turned his back on her to stir the eggs, and for a few moments the only sound in the room was the clank of the fork on the sides of the skillet. "How long do you think that agreement would last, Alex?" He sounded almost sad.

Alex said stiffly, "Are you saying he was lying?"

"Not exactly. Neville's an expert at selective truth. But even if he agreed to that deal, how long do you think it would be before Neville and company started chipping away at the promises? 'Just this one case, Kane...just this one trip...just this one weekend.' And before long it'd be the same as before."

"But—"

"I'm staying here, Alex, where I can live like a human being. In Duluth, I'm five minutes from work, ten blocks from the health club, fifteen steps from the lake. I can practice law when I like and still go fishing every day after work. If I returned to Pence Whitfield, inside of six weeks I'd be back in the same old meat grinder."

Alex's head was spinning. "Last night, you said we could make it work."

"We can." His voice was almost grim. "If you want to stay here with me, you're welcome."

Her hands were clenched together, shaking, as she watched her dream disappear in a puff of smoke. He'd said he cared about her, and she supposed it had been the truth. He did care, but only up to the point where caring interfered with his plans....

"I thought you meant a compromise," she said bitterly. "But what you really meant was that I'd have to give in to your point of view, wasn't it?"

"I haven't made any secret of where I stand, Alex. You chose to deceive yourself about it, but that's not my problem."

She jumped up, too agitated to sit any longer. "But we can have it all, Kane. More time off for both of us, more freedom to set our schedules—all the things you were talking about. They'd have agreed to the conditions."

"For the moment maybe."

"It's not a scheme, Kane! They want you back so desperately they'd have given me anything I wanted, too."

He turned to look at her. His eyes were icy. "And all you had to do was deliver the goods. Me."

Alex bit her lip. He sounded so cold, so hard. She'd never heard that tone in his voice before. And the way he looked ...

Kane said quietly, "I must admit Neville chose his bait well."

She blinked. She hadn't the foggiest idea what he meant, but she knew from the chill in his voice that it was no compliment. "What ... ?"

"Don't play dumb, Alex. Why do you think they sent you, anyway? Why not someone who was on my team, who could cite particular areas in which I was missed? You don't even know what's going on in that whole end of the practice."

She gulped. "They sent me because I had a legitimate reason to be in Duluth."

Kane shook his head. "They sent you because Neville Morgan suspected that every time I looked at you I wouldn't be thinking about law." His voice was almost brutal. "Be sure to tell him for me that the bait was very attractive. But unfortunately for him, I didn't bite quite hard enough to get hooked."

Alex felt as if a rock was resting on her chest, a boulder just large enough to crush the life from her as slowly and painfully as possible.

Bait. When he looked at her that was what he saw—a tasty morsel dangled invitingly in front of him. A morsel he could take as he had last night—or leave without a second thought.

If you want to stay with me, you're welcome, he'd said almost carelessly. He'd admitted he found her attractive. But her dreams of having more than that—of the possibility that someday she might be that best friend he wanted, the woman he'd marry...

A fish doesn't fall in love with the worm that entices it, she told herself bitterly. And that was exactly what she had been—an unwitting worm. Neville Morgan had surveyed his prey and chosen his bait with care. He had sent her out just as deliberately as a trout fisherman cast his line.

And she had performed exactly as she was supposed to, Alex thought. Right down to going to bed with him last night.

She'd never once seen that she was being used. Even when Neville Morgan had made that offhand remark about his daughter, Alex had not realized the same principle applied to her.

She said bitterly, "You'd better watch out, Kane. I'm not the only fly in Neville Morgan's tackle box. He said to tell you if you want to marry his daughter he'll lock her up till she agrees."

She turned on her heel and stalked up the stairs with all the dignity she could muster. It wasn't much, and she cursed herself as she yanked on her clothes. Why had she even tried to have the last word? All she'd succeeded in doing was to make it sound as if she'd been a willing participant in this scheme.

And wasn't that better than the alternative? she asked herself. Wasn't it more bearable to look like a scheming harpy than an utter fool? A fool who had mistaken sexual attraction for love and thought that if two people cared about each other...

His definition of caring was different from hers, that was obvious. Kane had merely meant that if it wasn't any trouble for him, he'd be happy to have her around.

Still, a tiny bit of her refused to give up the hope that he might be waiting when she came downstairs. That he might have calmed down, thought it over and reconsidered the idea of compromise.

But the kitchen was empty. On the stove, the eggs sizzled threateningly and started to smolder. Alex turned off the burner and slid the skillet aside.

From the window a movement caught her eye. Kane was standing on the top of the seawall staring out over the lake.

As she watched, he raised his hand and threw something out toward the water. For an instant, Alex was mystified, and then she remembered the agate he'd brought up from the beach. The stone he'd found for her, the special stone that symbolized their night together. She'd left it on the corner of the breakfast table, and now he'd thrown it back where it had come from. The lake that was at the center of the whole problem. . . .

Alex swallowed hard. As quietly as she could, she stole out to her car and drove away. And she cried as she drove back to the Guest House to pick up the rest of her belongings.

She had no trouble at all finding her way out of Duluth. It wasn't such a complicated little town, after all, she admitted. Kane had said once that Duluth was a threat to her peace of mind. She hadn't understood then what he was saying, but now she did. He thought she had found the town, and the way of life it represented, threatening because it was attractive, because it challenged her devotion to Pence Whitfield and to her career. So Kane had seen her habit of getting lost as a subconscious reaction, a way to protect herself from questions she didn't want to face.

He was probably right about the reasons she'd gotten lost, Alex thought, but fortunately he hadn't carried the logic all the way through. It wasn't Duluth she had found so fascinating. It was Kane. With Kane beside her, the isolated little house on the north shore would be paradise all year round.

She'd rolled down all the car windows, hoping the fresh air would help stop her tears. The air already held the nip of autumn. The twelve days of summer that Kane had joked about were nearly at an end.

And Alex's summer's worth of romance had been over even faster.

THE WHOLE ATMOSPHERE of Pence Whitfield seemed different somehow, even though Alex knew quite well that the decor, the faces and the pace of the office staff were all precisely the same as they'd been two weeks before. It was almost the close of the regular business day when she came in, but one would not know it from the unceasing hum of activity at Pence Whitfield. The day support staff might be ready to go home, but the swing shift was just gearing up.

In the small office just outside Alex's, her secretary set aside a folder and gave Alex a smile that held a great deal of relief, but no surprise. "I expected you'd be back today," Sharon said. "The last time I called the Guest House, they told me you'd checked out."

There wasn't a hint of reproof in her voice, but Alex found herself feeling guilty, anyway. There'd been three messages from Sharon when she went back to the Guest House to pack her things, but she hadn't returned the calls. The last thing she had needed right then was to talk to anyone at Pence Whitfield.

"I hope it wasn't critical," Alex said. "I just wanted to get on the road and get home." She snapped on the lights in her office. "Come on in and let's catch up."

Even her own office looked unfamiliar to her now. Its tailored perfection seemed stark and severe when compared with the ruffled elegance of her room at the Guest House. And it looked stiflingly formal when she remembered the simplicity of Fiona's clinic.

Sharon followed her into the room with a legal pad and sat down beside the desk. "First, and probably most important, Mr. Morgan wants a report on his desk in the morning."

Alex smothered a sigh. It could have been worse, she thought. He could have been waiting for her right now. "Then I'd better get to work," she said. "What else happened while I was gone? Business as usual?"

In fact, it was nearly ten that evening before Alex left the office, her reports finally done. She was not the last to leave; the lights were still burning brightly along the corridor that housed the mergers-and-acquisitions wing, and she knew several of the public-finance attorneys were closeted in one of the conference rooms, because she saw a cart loaded with food being wheeled in.

She was dead tired, but she didn't want to go back to her silent apartment. The rooms would be suffocatingly stuffy from being closed up for almost two weeks. There would be mail to deal with, laundry to sort and send out, a refrigerator full of old food to throw away. And she didn't want to be alone, with time to think.

Her self-esteem was still vibrating from the blows she had taken that morning. How could she have been so naive, failing to see what Neville Morgan was up to? "Neville Morgan didn't get where he is by being idealistic," she had told Paul Wintergreen just yesterday. She hadn't realized when she said it just how correct she'd been. There was no one the man wouldn't use if it suited his purpose. Alex had just happened to be the most promising lure he had available. So he'd sent her to Duluth in the hope she'd be enough to entice Kane into following her back.

But it hadn't worked. Not that she hadn't innocently given it her best shot. Alex shuddered at the thought of how well she had played her part.

Neville Morgan had handled her perfectly. He had foreseen precisely how she would think and act. His mistake had been in underestimating Kane's determination and overestimating the extent of his attraction to Alex. Kane had not been the helpless moth circling the irresistible flame, as Neville Morgan had hoped, after all.

That was what really hurt, Alex thought. Not that she wanted Kane to be helpless, exactly, but it wounded her to know he could so easily put her aside. Kane had said himself that he found her attractive, that even at that Christmas party he'd wanted to get to know her better....

No, Alex reminded herself, what Kane had said was that he'd wanted to kiss her. It was an entirely different thing. Nearly everyone at the party had been making fools of themselves; stealing a kiss was small potatoes.

And he hadn't pursued the desire, anyway, because business had been more important. Of course, when she'd made herself available and convenient, he had been happy to play along....

And so for the past two weeks he'd enjoyed himself in her presence. Perhaps he'd even been amused by the way she'd pursued him. But she didn't really matter to him, or he never would have turned his back on what they'd shared.

SHE WAS ALMOST at Jacobi's before she even realized that's where she was headed. And when she walked into the restaurant and saw one of the waiters behind the bar, instead of her father, she nearly panicked. She could count on her fingers the number of times in her whole life she'd seen someone other than Gus behind that bar.

"Boy, am I glad you're here, Alex," the waiter said.

"Where's Gus?" she demanded.

"Upstairs. He hasn't been feeling well for a couple of days."

"And nobody let me know?" Her voice was taut. "He's passed out so many of my business cards that I'd think everyone in the neighborhood would know where to find me."

"He didn't want us to bother you, Alex. Said you had enough on your mind."

She bit her lip and forced herself to take the stairs slowly, instead of bounding up them as she'd have liked. Gus, sick? It had been years since he'd missed even a day of work.

The apartment was dim. The only light came from the television set, which cast a flickering bluish light across the recliner where Gus Jacobi lay. His eyes were closed and his mustache drooped dispiritedly.

Alex's high heels clicked against the hardwood floor despite her best efforts to be silent, and Gus sat up abruptly. "Alex! What are you... Those lily-livers downstairs called you, didn't they?"

She stood over him, hands on hips. "Why didn't you want them to let me know you were sick, Papa?"

He didn't meet her eyes. "I'm not sick. I've got a touch of flu, that's all. No sense in dragging you back from the ends of the earth. You've got more important things to do than hold my hand."

"No, I don't, Papa." She pulled a chair up to the recliner. The tightness around her heart relaxed a little. He sounded a little weak, she thought, but otherwise he was Gus Jacobi at his best. Perhaps it *was* only flu.

"How about that project in Duluth? You can just leave it hanging like that?"

"It's done." She laid her fingers lightly against the back of his hand. "And in any case, it's not as important to me as you are."

She expected some quick answer about hard work, because that was the sort of thing he always said. But Gus didn't reply. A moment later, he turned his hand to make his fingers interlace with hers. It was all the answer Alex needed.

Thank you for that much, Kane, she thought. *Someday when Gus is gone, at least I won't have the same re-*

grets you have about Tess. I'll know I tried my best to have time for him....

She kissed his forehead and said as casually as she could, "My bedroom is still set up, isn't it? How would you like to have me around this weekend? The whole weekend?"

He didn't answer. There was something in his eyes that looked suspiciously like moisture, but everyone knew that Gus Jacobi didn't cry.

NEVILLE MORGAN WAS NOT pleased with her reports. Alex knew it the moment she walked into his office on Friday afternoon in response to his secretary's summons. But then, she'd hardly expected him to be delighted with the news that Kane wasn't coming back.

What she hadn't been quite prepared for was his complete disregard of Kane. Instead, he wanted to talk about Geoffrey Wintergreen's estate. And he made no effort to disguise his displeasure about her advice to Paul.

"I think you've jumped to conclusions," he said, snapping a finger against the report that lay open on his desk blotter. "Based on the minimal evidence you uncovered, to have advised Paul to agree to a settlement is premature, to say the least."

Alex folded her hands on her knee. "I didn't suggest that he offer a settlement. I advised him to wait, rather than invest any more money into a search at this time."

"If we don't search those files, we won't have the necessary information to judge the strength of any claim that may come up, Alexandra."

He sounded as if he was talking to a freshman law student, Alex thought resentfully. "It's possible I may have been in error," she said stiffly, "but I used my best professional judgment, Mr. Morgan. I honestly believed that was why you wanted me to go to Duluth in the first place. If you intended someone to spend two weeks up there shuffling papers and no more, you could have sent my secretary.''

Neville Morgan smiled a little. There was no humor in the expression. ''Shall we consider that unsaid, Alexandra?''

She put her chin up, but she had no opportunity to speak before he cleared his throat and went on.

''I take a great deal of the responsibility myself, of course,'' he said. ''Sending you up to talk to Kane was my mistake.''

Startled, Alex said, ''I don't quite—''

''It sounds as if his particular brand of liberal thinking is infectious. Kane was never much of a team player, which is the main reason he hasn't been offered a partnership before now. But this newest philosophy of his is a big departure from his usual harebrained notions.'' He shook his head sadly. ''I must admit, however, that I'm disappointed in you, Alexandra. I didn't expect that *you* would be taken in.''

What nonsense, she thought. He could probably even look her straight in the eye and tell her that he wasn't desperate to get Kane back, after all, and that he'd never, ever considered using her....

She actually thought about telling him all those things and then walking out of the office. She could just pick up her briefcase and...

...go back to Duluth, she mused dreamily.

If you want to stay here with me, you're welcome, Kane had said.

I wonder what he would do, Alex thought, *if I just showed up on his doorstep.*

Then she sighed. He had issued the invitation, all right, but there'd been a coolness in his voice that said he didn't really care what her answer was, because he didn't really care about *her*.

It was a long way from how she wanted him to feel. She wanted him to love her with every thread of his being—the way she loved him. She couldn't bear to be only a mild distraction, entertainment while he waited for the right woman to come along, the woman he could really love.

And she knew now she could never be that woman. If she had fit at all into his image of the woman he wanted, Kane wouldn't have ignored her for practically two years after that stupid Christmas party. He wouldn't have so carelessly tossed out the invitation to stay in Duluth. He wouldn't have made it so painfully apparent that his choices were made and that he didn't intend to consider her wishes, her desires, her ambitions.

"Alexandra?" Neville Morgan's voice was sharp. "I can count on you this weekend, then? There's a lot of work to do to get this new project off the ground."

She slid to the edge of her chair and smiled at him. "I'm sorry," she said politely, "but I've made plans for the weekend. I'll be happy to start on Monday morning."

She wasn't exactly walking on air as she returned to her office, but she felt better for standing up to him. She knew what to expect from Neville Morgan now. Despite his unscrupulous side, she could still work with him, and probably even learn from him. But she would not be used again.

She had a job she still loved, she reminded herself. She had the beginning of a new relationship with her father. She had a better understanding of her own strength. And as for the other things she wanted, the things she could not have . . .

If I can't have what I'd like, she told herself, *then I'll simply make the best of what I have.*

CHAPTER TEN

NEVILLE MORGAN'S new project was complicated. The client was setting up a family trust and was determined to cover every conceivable eventuality for as many years as he could possibly tie things up. But the law set limits on how long a trust could endure; Alex's part in the whole affair was to research every credible way there was to extend that period of time.

It was a necessary but very boring kind of law, the type of assignment Alex had thought she was past now that there were younger associates in the firm. But she held her tongue, instead of arguing about it, and holed up in the law library to do her research. If Neville Morgan thought he needed to make a point by putting her on probation and forcing her to prove herself all over again after the twin fiascos in Duluth, she supposed it was his right.

The truth was, however, that Alex still refused to believe she could have accomplished anything more where Kane was concerned. She had done her best with the inadequate information she'd been given, but the effort had been doomed from the start. If the senior partners thought a different kind of approach would convince Kane to come back, let them try it.

As for the Wintergreen estate, she would stand by her advice forever, unless conditions changed—which so far they had not. And though Neville Morgan disagreed with her judgment, Paul Wintergreen seemed to approve, even after he'd had a chance to think everything through. Just yesterday, as a matter of fact, he had called her with a couple of questions about the estate. He'd wanted *her* opinion, not Neville Morgan's.

And what if those disagreements meant she might never get her partnership? The prospect still stung, but not as much as she'd expected it to. At least she'd be able to face herself in the mirror and know she'd done her best. And there might be compensations. She and Gus had had a wonderful weekend. If only Kane had been able to see that it was possible to compromise, after all....

No, she told herself. The rift between them was wider than that, for Kane hadn't even wanted to try to find a middle ground.

Alex realized abruptly that her mind was wandering yet again. She looked down at the fine print of the case she'd been reading. She was halfway through the argument, but not a word of it looked familiar.

She pushed the book away and rubbed her temples. It was so difficult to concentrate; Pence Whitfield's library was almost too quiet and isolated. There wasn't even a window to provide a sense of time passing.

Not that it would matter, she told herself. If there were noises or other people running in and out, she'd be complaining about that. The truth was she just couldn't seem to discipline herself anymore.

The door opened. "Alex?"

She tugged the book back into place. "I thought I told you I wasn't to be disturbed, Sharon."

"I didn't think you'd mind for this."

Alex looked up, intrigued despite herself. Sharon was practically invisible behind a wall of red roses. She set the big crystal vase down at Alex's elbow, and the heavy perfume wrapped itself around Alex like a blanket. The dew-flecked petals were such a dark red that the hearts of the flowers were almost black.

Red roses, Alex thought, and a husky voice whispered again in her memory, *I didn't have a red rose for your pillow this morning . . .*

"Twenty-four of them," Sharon said. There was a twinkle in her eye. "I couldn't believe it, so I counted. What a business trip that must've been."

Alex's hands were trembling as she reached for the tiny envelope tucked in amid the green stems.

"I know you said you didn't want to take telephone calls," Sharon went on, "but since I've already interrupted—"

"No calls," Alex said automatically. The envelope was sealed. She slid a fingernail under the edge of the flap.

"Kane Forrestal is holding. He said it was important that he talk to you, and I thought—"

Alex pushed her chair back. "Yes," she said. Her voice cracked and she hastily cleared her throat. "I'll talk to him, of course."

Red roses . . . and now a phone call. Her pulses skittered; she could feel excitement pounding in her veins.

She crumpled the envelope in her palm. She certainly couldn't leave that—or the roses—in the library, where any member of the staff might wander in and get curious. Back in her office, she didn't bother to walk all the way around to her chair; she perched on the corner of the desk, instead. As she waited for Sharon to transfer the call, she tugged the tiny card out of the envelope.

What had he written on it? she wondered. She shouldn't expect anything too fantastic, of course, for this bouquet would have been wired, not sent direct. He'd probably limited himself to ordinary sentiments, so the message wouldn't get garbled or serve to amuse every person who handled the order....

Very ordinary sentiments, she thought in astonished chagrin. She held the card at arm's length and read it again. Yes, it really did say simply, "Many thanks." And it had been signed, not by Kane, but by Paul Wintergreen.

She tried to swallow her disappointment, but her throat was too tight and raw.

It was lovely of Paul, she told herself bleakly, to thank her for dropping everything yesterday to answer his questions. It was a gesture she would have appreciated a great deal if she hadn't been so foolish as to jump to other conclusions. Red roses, indeed! As if red roses could have only one meaning....

The small blue light on the telephone blinked steadily at her. Kane was there, at least, she reminded herself. She picked up the receiver. Her fingers were trembling.

"Alex," he said, "how are you?"

The vibration of that gloriously rich voice rippled through every cell of her body. *I'm terrible,* she thought. *I'm lonely and I'm hurting and I wish you cared.*

"Busy," she said.

"I gathered that. Your secretary must have had to go to Timbuktu to get you."

There seemed no doubt in his mind that no matter how busy she was, she'd take a call from him. She was annoyed to have to admit he was right about that; she'd jumped at the chance to talk to him.

"Sorry to keep you waiting," she said crisply. "What can I do for you?"

"Fiona turned that trust case you were looking at over to me. She said you had some insight on how to handle it."

Of course it wouldn't be anything personal, Alex thought. The back of her eyelids stung a little. "Nothing I haven't already told Fiona."

Her palms were sticky with perspiration. She reached for a tissue and carefully mopped moisture off the telephone.

Kane was silent.

How long was she going to let this go on? Alex asked herself. "I'm sure you can handle a case like that without my help, Kane. You're a perfectly competent attorney." As soon as the words were out, she regretted giving in to the hurtful little imp in the back of her brain. Quietly she added, "If I have any brainstorms, I'll let you know. But I really am too busy to give it much thought."

"Is Neville cracking the whip? How did he take the news?"

"Not well," Alex said honestly.

"Should I brace myself for a string of senior partners coming to visit?"

The prospect didn't seem to trouble him, Alex noticed. And why should it? "I wouldn't know. I'll warn you if I hear anything."

"Thanks. I'll take you out to dinner next time you're up this way."

Just what I need, Alex thought. "I'll call you if I get back to town."

There was a tiny silence. "If? You'll still be dealing with Paul Playboy, won't you?"

She looked at Paul's card, lying crumpled on her desk blotter. "Oh, yes. Well...good luck with the case, Kane." She put the telephone down as gently as she could. She sat there quietly for a little while; her knees were shaking too much to support her.

If I thought he really wanted me, Alex told herself, *I'd be back in Duluth in a minute.* But the tone of that last question had sent a current of sadness through her. He'd been casual, nonchalant, unconcerned about whether she ever came back at all.

But at least he'd asked, something whispered deep inside her. Maybe she should go—just to be sure. Even if seeing him once more accomplished nothing else, it might force her to admit there wasn't anything in Duluth to long for. And that confession might help her put this pain to rest.

ALEX WAS ALREADY at the table studying the menu when Joanna Adler arrived. "Sorry to be late," Joanna said, shifting the bundle in her arms so she could pull the lightweight blanket away from the infant's face. "But upscale watering holes scowl on babies, so I thought we'd inflict him on the patrons for as short a time as possible."

The baby's big blue eyes blinked warily under the bright lights, and he screwed up his face and whimpered.

"Great way to start your first business lunch, Brandon," his mother told him. "Keep it up and you'll eat at home till you're eighteen." She settled the baby's seat into the chair between her and Alex.

Alex studied the dusting of freckles across Joanna's nose and cheeks. She'd never seen them before. "The baby's beautiful, Joanna. And you look—"

"Don't perjure yourself, Counselor. I'm not at all what you're used to seeing. No makeup, no great clothes. I don't have time anymore."

"As a matter of fact," Alex said, "the freckles are kind of cute."

"Not on a personnel director. They don't look professional. On a mommy, however..." Joanna took a deep breath. "I might as well break the big news right away. I'm not going back to work. And don't look at me that way, Alex."

Alex was stunned. Joanna, the consummate professional, giving up her job? Her reason for living?

Alex looked at the baby again. He yawned, and something inside her twisted. *If he were mine,* she thought, *what would I do? If things had been different in Duluth...*

"And don't ask me what happened," Joanna said, sounding almost irritable, "because I don't know. But every time I think of someone else seeing his first smiles and his first steps, I just start to howl."

"You fell in love with him," Alex said softly. "I can see why." She handed a wrapped box across the table.

"Another gift?"

"The other one didn't really count."

Joanna gave her a puzzled look and lifted out the neatly pressed pink-and-blue quilt. "You made this, Alex? I had no idea you did things like this. It's adorable. I'll wrap him in it for his christening." She reached across the table for Alex's hand. "I know it's a lot to ask. You're so busy. But I'd really like you to be his godmother, Alex, if you can fit it into your schedule."

A warm rush of pleasure swept over Alex, the thrill of being wanted and needed. How could she refuse her friend's invitation? In any case, she didn't want to. Her fingers closed tightly around Joanna's. "Don't fret about my schedule. I'll be there."

As Alex looked down at the baby with a new proprietary interest, a second less-welcome sensation flooded over her. This might be the only child ever to have a place in her life, she thought. A chill of regret settled deep into her bones.

The conflicting feelings made a bittersweet combination, and Alex was still trying to shake off her mood as she walked back to the office after lunch. It was silly to write off the idea of marriage and family, she told herself. She was young; there was plenty of time. There could be another man in her life someday. There could be a child....

But she knew it wasn't really a child she wanted. She'd never felt any particular urgency about having a family. Even now, with her uncomfortable new awareness that if Gus died she'd be left very much alone in the world, she hadn't considered a baby to be the answer.

Not unless it was Kane's baby. With him, she thought, everything was different.

She slipped through the unmarked door between the skywalk system and the back halls of Pence Whitfield, and turned into the corridor that led to the cluster of offices housing the estates-and-trusts division. The usual kaleidoscope of people formed and shifted in the hallway, and for a moment, as Alex looked through it, she thought she was imagining things.

At the far end of the hall, a man was standing by the receptionist's desk. A tall lean man in a precisely tailored three-piece gray suit, briefcase balanced on the edge of the desk. A man who looked just like Kane.

She stopped dead in her tracks. A law clerk who'd been behind Alex bumped into her and almost dropped his stack of books. Alex mumbled an apology, but she was only half-aware of what she was saying.

The receptionist will tell him I'm out, she thought. *Will he go away, or will he wait?*

She started walking slowly down the hall toward him, her steps jerky.

He was wearing the corporate uniform, she thought. She hadn't seen him in a three-piece suit in all the time she'd been in Duluth. She scarcely recognized him.

Kane nodded at the receptionist, lifted the alligator briefcase off the desk and turned away.

Alex's step quickened. He couldn't leave, she thought. He simply couldn't. "Kane!" she called.

He wheeled around, and his eyebrows arched as he saw her.

She wondered fleetingly why he looked surprised, and then answered her own question. *You fool,* she thought. *You're almost running down the hall. And what do you plan to do when you get to him? Throw yourself in his arms the way you did that night at Inglenook?*

He set his briefcase down beside a comfortable chair. He hadn't been leaving at all, Alex told herself. He was sitting down to wait.

But what was he waiting for? She reminded herself of the roses and the telephone call, and the way her hopes had been dashed. There were dozens of reasons he might visit Pence Whitfield. Most had nothing to do with her.

She took a deep breath and forced herself to walk slowly toward him with a friendly smile and out-stretched hand. "What a surprise, Kane." She was proud of herself; her voice held a good imitation of casual confidence. "I thought you were trying to stay as far away from Pence Whitfield as possible."

"I was," Kane said. He did not take her hand. "Things change. You don't sound happy, Alex."

Before she could decide whether to brightly deny the accusation or just burst into tears and admit the truth, the door to Neville Morgan's office opened. "Kane, my boy," he boomed. "Welcome back! Come on in and let's talk about how to patch up the damage you caused with all this nonsense of yours."

Alex stared at Kane, eyes wide, too astounded to make a sound. *Things change,* he'd said. Could he possibly mean what she thought he did?

Neville Morgan turned to her with a grin. "Congratulations, Alexandra," he said. "It seems you've underestimated your skills as a negotiator. Well, come along, Kane."

Kane gave her a crooked little smile. "We'll talk about it later, all right?" And then he was gone. Neville Morgan ushered him into the office and closed the door with a firm click.

Alex sat down on the arm of the nearest chair. If it hadn't happened to be there, she might have landed on the floor.

Kane was coming back. Back to Pence Whitfield, to a partnership or to whatever deal he and Neville Morgan would hammer out behind that closed door. But the basics of the agreement were already in place; that much was obvious from the good humor in Neville Morgan's voice. Kane was back.

But why? He'd meant what he said about staying in Duluth, Alex was certain of that. On that last morning at Inglenook, there'd been no reason for him to have kept his intentions from her. On the contrary, there had been every reason to tell the truth—especially if this was what he'd planned to do.

But he'd said he had no intention of ever coming back to Pence Whitfield. And Alex believed he meant it.

So what had changed his mind?

She ticked off the possibilities. It could not be an attack of self-doubt; he'd had plenty of time to work that out before he'd made his move in the first place. It was not conditions in Duluth, she was sure of that; she could not believe he and Fiona had quarreled.

Was it possible he was doing this for her?

The question was no more than a whisper at the back of her mind, a shocking query that carried incredible implications. And yet it was the only explanation that made any sense.

"It will all work out," he had said that single night they'd shared. "When two people care about each other..."

But the next morning Alex had declined his solution, and he had refused to consider hers. There had been no room left for compromise, no willingness to make concessions, and so they had parted.

But if this was his answer, now that he'd thought it over...

I've won, Alex thought numbly, *if he cares enough about me to do this for my sake.*

To come back to a job he hated, her conscience whispered. A job from which he'd said all the joy was gone. A job he'd referred to as a meat grinder.

They'd work out a deal, she told herself frantically. He knew he could have whatever he wanted. He could force the partners to agree to it.

His words spun through her mind. *How long do you think that agreement would last,* he'd said on that final morning at Inglenook, *before they started chipping away at the promises?*

It could be done, she told herself. She was doing it. She'd spent the weekend with her father. She'd had lunch with Joanna. She hadn't worked nearly as many hours this week, and no one had made a fuss about it...

...yet. The single word echoed in her head.

Deep in her heart, she knew that the freedom she'd claimed would not be easily maintained. There were so many special projects and important cases, and never enough hours to do all the work. And though Neville Morgan wasn't pushing her at the moment, she suspected he wasn't being patient so much as giving her all the rope she needed to hang herself. Eventually the pressure would be put on to do the job, no matter what.

And if that was the case in trusts and estates, with its relatively slow pace, how much more pressure would there be on Kane to perform, to pull off the deal no matter how many hours or miles or conferences it took?

Before she had consciously decided to act, she was inside Neville Morgan's office, pushing the door closed behind her. She could hear his secretary on the other side, pounding on it, as she leaned against the door to hold it shut.

Neville Morgan surged up from his chair. "This is a private conference, Alexandra!"

She ignored him. Breathlessly she said, "If you're doing this because of me, Kane—don't. Don't come back."

He stood up slowly and turned to face her. Amazement blazed in his eyes; it was the first time she'd ever seen him too surprised even to try to maintain a professional calm.

All right, she told herself. So she had misread the whole situation, and Kane didn't have her wishes in mind at all. But what she was trying to say was still just as true. He would never be happy at Pence Whitfield if his heart was somewhere else.

Neville Morgan's face was purple. "I've had enough impertinence from you, young woman! Get out of here!"

Alex didn't even look at him. Her eyes were still on Kane. "Don't do it," she whispered. She opened the door, slipped under the surprised secretary's arm and made a dash for her own office.

"What's all the fuss—" Sharon began as Alex burst in.

"No clients," Alex ordered. "No calls." She slammed the door of her office and stood in the middle of the room, her arms folded across her chest, shivering as if she was naked in the midst of a blizzard.

What a prime fool she'd made of herself this time, she thought.

The door eased open behind her, and Kane said, "Well, that's a comfort. I thought we might need the SWAT team just to get in."

Alex wheeled to face him. "I said I didn't want to be disturbed!"

"Don't blame Sharon. She told me you said no calls and no clients. Nothing about colleagues."

"You aren't one."

"What am I, then?" His tone was gentle, almost wheedling.

He would sound just the same if he was trying to talk me down off a window ledge, Alex thought bitterly.

"No answer?" Kane said. "All right. We can get back to that one later. I've got plenty of other questions to ask, instead. Why don't you want me to come back to the firm, Alex?"

"Don't cross-examine me, Kane." She turned her back on him, but she could see a flicker of movement from the corner of her eye. A moment later his jacket landed on the chair beside her. It was followed by his vest and then his tie.

"I'm quite comfortable now," he said calmly. "I can stay here just as long as you can."

She sneaked a look over her shoulder. He was sitting on the corner of her desk rolling up the sleeves of his white shirt to the elbow and looking as if he had moved in to stay. "Why, Alex?" he repeated calmly.

She smothered a sigh and turned to face him. "Because of everything you said. I just don't think you'd be happy. That's all."

And his next question, she thought, would probably be why she considered his happiness to be any of her business. She should have refused to say anything at all.

"Would that matter to you?" he asked softly. "Whether I was happy?"

Alex flashed a bright meaningless smile. She didn't quite meet his eyes. "Of course. I always want people to be happy."

"Isn't that nice of you." His voice was silky. He plucked a rose from the vase on her desk and buried his nose in it. "What about you, Alex?"

She shrugged and began to fiddle with the stack of law books on the credenza behind her desk. "Am I happy, you mean? I suppose."

"My guess is you don't have much of a future here anymore. Somehow I doubt Neville's the one who sent the roses."

She swallowed hard. She hadn't even allowed herself to think about what she would do now. When it came to jumping out of the frying pan into the fire, she was a champion. "Don't worry about my future."

"If you're allowed to fret about my career, then I can fret about yours." He'd moved closer; Alex could feel a warning tingle in her bones and smell the drugging scent of the rose in his hand. "I can't see Neville offering you a partnership after that performance in his office a few minutes ago."

"It doesn't matter." She knew she sounded tired, but she didn't care. "Being a partner isn't the most important thing in my life anymore."

"That depends, don't you think?"

Alex knew he was smiling, even though she wasn't looking at him. She could hear it in his voice.

"What do you mean?"

"On what kind of partnership we're talking about."

Her heart ached with longing, but she couldn't allow herself to hope, for it hurt too much when hope was smashed. "If you're offering me a job at Fiona's clinic—"

"No." He tossed the rose aside, then put both hands on her shoulders and turned her to face him. "Though if that's what you want . . ."

Alex's heart sank. Once she had looked down her nose at Fiona's clinic. Now a job there seemed like heaven on earth—but only if she could have Kane, too.

Kane planted both thumbs beneath her chin and forced her face up till her eyes met his. "I mean a legal partnership—and a personal one. Marry me, Alex."

She gasped, then started to cough.

He patted her on the back for half a minute and finally protested, "Dammit, Alex, will you stop? I never thought that when I got around to proposing to a woman she'd choke to death!"

She managed to catch her breath and said hoarsely, "It's because you know how I feel and you're sorry for me, isn't it?"

Kane swore under his breath and pulled her into his arms. "I've never thought you were silly, Alex. But that particular statement deserves harsh treatment." His mouth came down on hers in a long demanding kiss that wiped out her ability to think, to move, to do anything but feel his warmth and strength and the rush of love that surged through her.

He held her away from him and said, "Do you still think..." He stopped, then went on gruffly, "Oh, the hell with it. Since I've got your attention for the moment, I'm going to take advantage of it."

This kiss was gentler, softer, and even more devastating. By the time he pulled his mouth away, Alex's body was like a bowl of ice on a hot afternoon—slick and shivery and altogether out of control.

"Do you still think I want to marry you out of pity?" Kane's voice had a rough edge.

Alex shook her head and buried her face in his shoulder. Hot happy tears burned her eyelids.

"When you came bursting into Neville's office," he confessed softly, "I thought for just a moment you meant that you didn't care for me, and no matter what I did, that wouldn't change."

She looked up at him, eyes wide. "No. Oh, no."

"I came in here and saw the roses, and that didn't help. But then you said you wanted me to be happy...." He put his cheek down against her hair. "That's what I want for you, too, Alex. What you said that last morning, about me expecting you to give up everything you wanted so I could have my way, set me back on my heels. It was true. And when I called you about Fiona's case and realized how unhappy you were..."

"I was very careful what I said that day." Alex's voice was muffled by the material of his shirt.

He smiled a little. "You tried, I'll grant you. But I knew you were miserable nevertheless. That's when I realized that no matter what you chose to do, I had destroyed your career. You didn't want to leave the firm, but the partners would never again trust you completely.

And I couldn't bear to do that to you. So I started looking for a compromise."

"There isn't one," Alex said.

"That's what I concluded. So I called Neville."

She raised her head. "You'd honestly come back to Pence Whitfield for me?"

"Yes. I would. If that's what you want, we'll go into Neville's office and fling ourselves at his feet and plead temporary insanity."

"You wouldn't be happy, Kane."

His arms tightened around her. "Maybe I wouldn't be ecstatic," he admitted. "But I think I could be reasonably content—as long as I had you."

"Fiona wouldn't be very happy."

"True. But she'd get over it. Well, Alex? What's it going to be?"

She gave in. "Not Pence Whitfield, I think. We couldn't make much of a deal if we were groveling at Neville's feet. Besides, you're right. I don't have a future here. Not because of that outburst this afternoon, either, but because I've changed. I want different things now, Kane."

He smiled down at her. "I thought perhaps you did," he said. "I began to suspect you'd changed the first night we had dinner together."

"How?" she asked softly. Had it been so obvious even then that she was falling in love?

"Oh, because you saw instinctively that we were really on the same side of the question."

"I just didn't know yet which side that was," Alex said ruefully.

"Something like that." He stroked her hair with a gentle fingertip. "When you first turned up in Duluth, I tried to stay away from you altogether. I was afraid of you.''

"Afraid? Of me?''

"There's this incredible innocent magic about you, Alex, and it drives me crazy.''

"Is that what makes me good bait?'' she asked flatly.

"I'm sorry I said that. I always knew that you had no idea what Neville was up to. I was hurt that morning, and so I struck out at you.'' He kissed the end of her nose and added, ''But you're right—it *is* what makes you so alluring. You do remember that Christmas party, don't you?''

"I seem to recall it,'' Alex said cautiously.

"We spent half the evening in a little nook off to the side of the ballroom, and all you wanted to talk about was the Reynolds case. You didn't even notice that I was practically drooling over you.''

"I noticed that two minutes later you were dancing with Lisle Morgan,'' she admitted.

"You did?'' He sounded delighted. "I actually thought once about marrying her, you know. That's what first scared me into reconsidering my entire life—because I realized the only reason I was attracted to the woman was that I wouldn't have to waste any time courting her. She wouldn't have had to be locked in her room, that's for sure. Then you came along—and you were only interested in business.''

"I suppose I thought that was the best way to get your attention.''

"Well, you did too good a job of it. You made it plain you weren't at all interested in me.''

"Oh,'' she said.

"When you first turned up in Duluth I knew very well I ought to stay away from you, but I couldn't. And you had changed. You were softer somehow, and at least you noticed whenever I made a remark with a double meaning."

"Who could have missed it?" Her tone was almost tart.

"You would have been oblivious before," he said. "Before I quite knew what had hit me, I had fallen completely in love with you. I was certain you'd come to see that what I was offering was what you wanted, too, but when you threw it back in my face that last morning . . ."

"I was an idiot." Her voice was muffled.

Kane kissed her temple. "If I hadn't come to Minneapolis today, Alex, would you have called me when you came up to see Paul next time?"

She toyed with a couple of answers, and then reminded herself that all she needed now was to tell the truth. "Yes. Because no matter how much it hurt me, not seeing you would have been worse."

"It wouldn't have hurt," he said huskily. "I promise you that." He fumbled in his pants pocket. "I brought this for you."

Swinging like a hypnotist's charm from a delicate silver chain was the agate he'd found for her on Inglenook's beach. Alex's hand closed around it. "You didn't throw it away," she whispered.

"I tried. I couldn't let go of the damned thing. I guess even then I hoped you'd want to wear it someday."

She turned around and bent her head. He fastened the slim silver chain around her neck and let his lips rest against the catch.

"Where shall we go on our honeymoon?" he asked, turning her back around to face him.

"I don't care. Can we even manage one? I don't have a job at all, and you don't have much of one."

Kane laughed and kissed her. "Of course we can have a honeymoon. We can go anywhere in the world on my frequent-flier miles." He pulled her close, till her head was tucked neatly under his chin. "And don't panic about what we're going to live on. I'm not particularly fond of poverty myself."

She slanted a look up at him. "Meaning?"

"I've still got a nice stock portfolio, accumulated over the past few years when I didn't have any time to spend what I was making. Aunt Tess left me a bit, too, so I couldn't use money as an excuse for dwindling into a one-dimensional overachiever."

"'Do what you should do,'" Alex quoted softly. "'Not necessarily what you're capable of.' Now I know what she meant. Just because you're good at one tiny bit of law doesn't mean you should do only that. There are other important things in the world, even if they're important only to you."

The way he smiled at her made Alex feel as if she'd won an award.

"Fiona's made a mint over the years in her regular practice," he went on, "which is the one she's turning over to me. So if you'd like to practice law, you've got a partner. If you want to raise flowers, instead, I can still afford you."

"I want to be partners, Kane. I think I've already got one client to bring into the firm with me, too."

Kane looked suspiciously at the roses on her desk. "Paul Playboy, I suppose? He'd better be no more than a client."

Alex hugged him close. "Of course not. You'll be my best friend, and my lover...."

"And sometimes, no doubt, a bloody nuisance."

She smiled, remembering. "I won't mind," she promised softly. "I do love you, you know."

He said thoughtfully, "Of course you realize that's probably just the lake effect at work."

She frowned at him.

"That's why we're going back there," he added softly. "Because I love you, too. And I want to make sure neither of us ever gets over it."

Let

HARLEQUIN ROMANCE®

take you

BACK TO THE

Come to the Circle Q Ranch, near Yerington, Nevada!

Meet "cattle king" Zack Quinn, a wealthy and well-connected rancher. And meet Alexandria Duncan, small-business owner and surrogate parent....

Read THE RANCHER AND THE REDHEAD
by Rebecca Winters, September's Back to the Ranch title!
Available in September wherever Harlequin books are sold.

**Relive the romance...
Harlequin and Silhouette
are proud to present**

by Request

A program of collections of three complete novels by the most requested authors with the most requested themes. Be sure to look for one volume each month with three complete novels by top name authors.

In June: **NINE MONTHS** Penny Jordan
                                       Stella Cameron
                                       Janice Kaiser

Three women pregnant and alone. But a lot can happen in nine months!

In July: **DADDY'S
               HOME**   Kristin James
                                       Naomi Horton
                                       Mary Lynn Baxter

Daddy's Home ... and his presence is long overdue!

In August: **FORGOTTEN
                PAST**   Barbara Kaye
                                       Pamela Browning
                                       Nancy Martin

Do you dare to create a future if you've forgotten the past?

Available at your favorite retail outlet.

HARLEQUIN   Silhouette